Saki

The Complete Annotated Reginald Stories

containing

Reginald and *Reginald in Russia*

edited

and with an introduction by

Bruce Gaston

FAVORITEN
PRESS

Front matter and notes © 2015 by Bruce Gaston and the Favoriten Press.

All rights reserved. No part of this publication may be reproduced, distributed, or transmitted in any form or by any means, including photocopying, recording, or other electronic or mechanical methods, without the prior written permission of the editor and/or publisher, except in the case of brief quotations embodied in critical reviews and certain other noncommercial uses permitted by copyright law.

To contact the editor, please use bruce.gaston@as.uni-heidelberg.de.

Text set in Storm Type Foundry's Lido STF.

Cover created from graphic elements designed by Freepik.com and the Cormorant font designed by Christian Thalmann of Catharsis Fonts (christian.d.thalmann@gmail.com).

Contents

Introduction	v
Chronology	xiii
Suggestions for further reading	xvii
General reading	xvii
On Saki	xvii
Editor's note	xix

Reginald (1904)   3
- Reginald 3
- Reginald on Christmas Presents 6
- Reginald on the Academy 9
- Reginald at the Theatre 12
- Reginald's Peace Poem 15
- Reginald's Choir Treat 18
- Reginald on Worries 20
- Reginald on House-Parties 23
- Reginald at the Carlton 25
- Reginald on Besetting Sins 29
- Reginald's Drama 31
- Reginald on Tariffs 35
- Reginald's Christmas Revel 38
- Reginald's Rubaiyat 41

The Innocence of Reginald 45

Reginald in Russia (1910)   **51**
Reginald In Russia 51
The Reticence Of Lady Anne 54
The Lost Sanjak 58
The Sex That Doesn't Shop 64
The Blood-Feud Of Toad-Water 66
A Young Turkish Catastrophe 70
Judkin Of The Parcels 72
Gabriel-Ernest. 74
The Saint And The Goblin 81
The Soul of Laploshka 84
The Bag 89
The Strategist 94
Cross Currents. 98
The Baker's Dozen 105
The Mouse 110

Introduction

When he published the story 'Reginald' in 1901, Hector Hugh Munro was thirty years old and had already experienced a couple of false starts in his efforts to establish himself in a profession. Service in the colonial police force in Burma had been cut short by malaria, and his first book, an historical work entitled *The Rise of the Russian Empire* (1900), which had taken three years of research in the British Library, had been reviewed politely but did not sell well.

However, by the following year it looked as if Munro had finally found his way onto the right path for his talents. He had scored a success with a series of political sketches which parodied *Alice in Wonderland* to satirise the topsy-turvy world of British politics. Illustrated in an appropriate style by the popular political cartoonist Francis Carruthers Gould and published in the respected and widely read *Westminster Gazette*, they proved so popular that they were collected and issued in book form. Although time has made their satirical intent inaccessible to anyone without a knowledge of Edwardian political personalities, Munro's near perfect imitation of the style and (il)logic of Lewis Carroll's tales still shines through today.

Over the next few years, he continued to publish short stories, more parodies (this time of Rudyard Kipling's *Just So Stories*), other satirical political sketches, and more tales of Reginald. Perhaps unsurprisingly for a young writer still feeling his way towards a style and subject matter, Munro often mixed his genres. Thus, a story like 'Reginald on Tariffs' took up a contemporary political debate, while 'Reginald's Drama' and 'Reginald's Rubaiyat' included elements of literary parody, mocking phenomena such as the new Ibsen-like type of drama or the mannered orientalist verse of the Victorian poet Edward FitzGerald.

It is worth pausing here to discuss FitzGerald and his most famous work, for it was this work that provided Munro's pen-name. FitzGerald (1809-1883), a gentleman poet and scholar, had discovered a set of Persian four-line poems (the technical name is 'rubáiyát') which had been written by an 11th century polymath named Omar Khayyám. FitzGerald translated and arranged a selection of these, publishing them in 1859. Taken up by Rossetti and Swinburne, among others, *The Rubáiyát of Omar Khayyám* became—after a slow start—extremely popular. In response, FitzGerald reworked and expanded it. In all, four editions were published within his lifetime and a fifth based on his notes was issued after his death. It was without doubt one of the literary hits of the later 19th century and extremely influential.

FitzGerald admitted that his translations were "very unliteral",[1] so much so that they are perhaps better described as paraphrases or imitations. His choice of quatrains to translate accentuated that aspect of Khayyám's work which expressed cynicism about divine providence and espoused a philosophy of "Carpe Diem" in the face of the mystery of death. Sandie Byrne comments "For an older generation it still had enough of a whiff of perfumed orientalism about it to feel faintly daring and advertise avant-garde taste, but the book was quite respectable and even scholarly, so for the younger generation, of course, it was a damp squib".[2] Munro had learned of the book from his sister and had even copied out some quatrains into his commonplace book (see page xx). Nevertheless, he had also clearly noted its potential to be exploited for satirical purposes. While writing his Alice parodies, he penned some quatrains

---

[1] Letter to E. B. Cowell, 3rd Sept. 1858.
[2] *The Unbearable Saki: The Work of H. H. Munro* (Oxford: Oxford Univ. Press, 2007), p. 103.

supposedly by a Middle Eastern poet named "Uttar Al Ghibe" in which he mocked the same politicians. Munro's biographer A. J. Langguth conjectures that it was this early work that led Munro to pick "Saki" as his *nom de plume*. The word is used in the FitzGerald versions (written there as "Sákí") and means "cupbearer". However, the pseudonym never subsumed the writer in the way that some pen-names do, and Munro continued to publish under his own name as well, a fact which may support the hypothesis that "Saki" was chosen quickly and casually. Later editions of his works tended to carry both names.

The negative example, as it were, of FitzGerald is one instance of a rejection of the Victorian era that also finds expression in the stories of Reginald, in which the younger generation clashes with its elders. Munro's professional writing life maps almost perfectly onto what is often inaccurately called the Edwardian Era (generally dated from 1901 to 1914, although King Edward VII actually died in 1910). The period was bounded at both ends by great upheavals: it began with the Boer War and the death of Queen Victoria and ended with the Irish Home Rule Crisis and the outbreak of the First World War.

The conclusion of the Boer War makes an appearance in an early Reginald story, 'Reginald's Peace Poem' (1902). More correctly, that date marked the end of the Second Boer War, the first having been fought in 1880-81. Both were struggles for control of the territory that is now South Africa. The Boers themselves were the descendants of Dutch settlers who had migrated inland, away from the British Cape Colony, and had set up two new states: the South African Republic (also known as the Transvaal Republic) and the Orange Free State. The discovery of diamonds and gold had attracted increasing numbers of British settlers into the Boers' territory, leading the latter to fear that they would soon be outnumbered in their new countries. Disputes over discrimination against the newcomers, the desire to exploit recently discovered diamonds and gold deposits, as well as more long-standing strategic considerations, resulted in a diplomatic stand-off only ended by the two republics declaring war on Great Britain in 1899. As the world's superpower, the British expected an easy victory, but the conflict turned into an expensive embarrassment. After an initial military campaign, the Boers resorted to guerrilla warfare, which the conventional tactics of the British Army found difficult to cope with. The Boers' resistance was only broken after the British implemented the twin policies (both highly controversial) of scorched earth tactics and internment camps for civilians. The Boers finally surrendered in 1902, to the relief of the British public. Their two territories were incorporated into the British Empire.

If the Boer War dominated the news when Munro began writing, another struggle, this one domestic, would remain in the public eye throughout his lifetime. The issue of votes for woman had been bubbling away since the 19th century, but the turn-of-the-century saw several developments that brought the subject to the forefront of public attention. The National Union of Women's Suffrage Societies had brought together a number of local pressure groups in 1897. In 1903 a new, more militant organisation, the Women's Social and Political Union, was founded by Emmeline Pankhurst. It was this latter group that pursued the tactics of civil disobedience, political violence and hunger strikes that most people today associate of the term "suffragette". Demonstrations and debates continued throughout the period when Munro was writing. His view on the topic can be ascertained from the political parable 'A Young Turkish Catastrophe', with its disparaging suggestion that women would simply vote the way their husbands directed them.

Yet despite the violence, threatened or real, of regional conflicts, Great-Power rivalry, suffragism, the Irish Home Rule crisis, and manifold other social, political and cultural upheavals, the popular image of the Edwardian period has long been of a kind of glorious summer garden party before the deluge of the Great War. After the conformity of the long Victorian Age there was a sense of freedom and change , particularly among the young. The Reginald stories perfectly capture this, with their cast of duchesses, social climbers, aunts and clergymen, and their background of the West End and the 'Season'. Above all, there is Reginald himself, the self-professed young man always ready to display the latest trends, be they in fashion, drama or opinions.

On turning to consider Reginald, we must confront an unspoken presence that hovers over these stories, namely that of Oscar Wilde. Reginald is a dandy, a single young man who disdains conventional morality in favour of the aesthetic, the Epicurean and the sartorial. While this figure was not an invention of Wilde, it was given great publicity by him, both through the characters in his works, such as *The Picture of Dorian Gray*, and through Wilde's own public image. Its scandalous nature was amplified after Wilde was imprisoned for homosexuality in 1895. The associations that the Reginald stories would have had for an audience at the time, not long after Wilde's early death at the age of 46, were therefore more outrageous than they seem today. It is of little use to speculate about the sexuality of Reginald himself or his creator. The circumstantial evidence is there for those who wish to make use of it. But in the case of Reginald, it must be remembered that everything he does or says is calculated for effect, one of the key elements of a dandy being his artificiality. Jessica R. Feldman comments on how the dandy is "a product of (his own) make-believe".[3] The pose and the mask adopted by a dandy are an affront to the bourgeois because they are unreal and therefore unserious, and this very unseriousness is perceived as an undermining of received truths. "Oh, you're simply exasperating. You've been reading Nietzsche till you haven't got any sense of moral proportion left. May I ask if you are governed by *any* laws of conduct whatever?" expostulates the Duchess, Reginald's conversational sparring partner, in 'Reginald at the Theatre'. Reginald is — naturally — ready with a riposte. Much of the pleasure of the stories comes from hearing conventional wisdom turned upon its head, and moreover from hearing it done so elegantly and wittily. The language

---

[3] *Gender On The Divide* (Ithaca, NY: Cornell Univ. Press, 1993), p. 2.

of the stories, while often indulging in the same kind of paradox that Wilde revelled in, is in no way inferior or just a pastiche of the older writer. Indeed, Munro's achievement in Reginald is to sustain a tone of voice and the flow of *bon mots* over the fifteen stories.

The title of Munro's second collection, *Reginald in Russia*, was presumably chosen to link back to his first collection. What exactly Reginald (who seemed rarely inclined to stray far from the fashionable spots of London) is doing in Russia is never explained. Nor is his complete disappearance from Munro's writings after this point. But *Reginald in Russia* contains Saki's first great stories. His tales of Reginald are amusing vignettes but they were of necessity limited in scope. In his second collection, the reader witnesses Munro honing in on the type of stories that he thereafter turned out with such apparent ease. In particular, 'Gabriel-Ernest', his story of a young werewolf, unites his key themes of polite society, savage nature and wild children. With consummate skill Munro manages to perfectly balance the comic and the horrific. The contrast between the dullard Van Cheele and his officious, do-gooder aunt on the one side and on the other the teenage Gabriel-Ernest, who lives in the forests and at night turns into a wolf to hunt, is an early example of Munro's tendency to present the ferocity of nature as in some way more honest than the (no less ruthless) social world. In his fiction, animals, like children, are depicted as more clear-sighted, being free of prejudices. However, Munro is in no way a believer in the essential innocence of childhood. As Reginald remarks, "people talk vaguely about the innocence of a little child, but they take mighty good care not to let it out of their sight for twenty minutes" ('The Innocence of Reginald'). In 'The Strategist', the young Rollo finds himself alone and opposed by three brothers, aware that the afternoon's entertainment will be violent and painful for him: when the boys are sent out of the room together, he is beaten first with a dog whip and then with a whalebone switch. But this is not a story of bullying, at least, not in the sense that Rollo is doomed to always be the victim. Rather, the story describes one episode in what Munro implies is a kind of Darwinian struggle for supremacy amongst children. It is made perfectly clear that it is not the violence *per se* that Rollo objects to, but the fact that he is outnumbered: "Two against three would have been exciting and possibly unpleasant; one against three promised to be about as amusing as a visit to the dentist." At the end of the story, Rollo manages to outwit his adversaries, and the similarity between the rules of the childhood world and the law of the jungle is made explicitly clear: "Rollo sank into a chair and smiled ever so faintly at the Wrotsleys, just a momentary baring of the teeth; an otter, escaping from the fangs of the hounds into the safety of a deep pool, might have given a similar demonstration of feelings."

When taken along with his elder sister Ethel's memoir of her brother,[4] in which she describes the practical jokes he played and how he loved a scrap to relieve his high spirits, the temptation to explain Munro's fiction in terms of his life becomes almost irresistible. Hector was the third child; he also had an elder brother, Charlie. There might have been a fourth child too, but their mother had miscarried and died after being charged by a cow while out strolling in the countryside. Hector was only two at the time, so it is unclear how much this bizarre mischance affected him. But when one thinks of the number of freak deaths involving animals in Munro's fiction, knowledge of this real-life parallel becomes even more unsettling.

Their father, a colonial official stationed in Burma, decided it would be better for three small, motherless children to live with their grandmother and two unmarried aunts in England. What seemed a sensible decision in fact took no account of the suitability (or rather the lack of it) of these family members. Their grandmother was strict only in regards to observance of the Sabbath, but the two aunts, Augusta and Charlotte, were bad-tempered tyrants, at war with the world and each other. Both seem to have subscribed to the Victorian view that children needed constant discipline and chastisement to curb their naturally evil natures. Hector was a sickly child and

---

[4] See 'Suggestions for further reading' on page xvii.

therefore spared many of the beatings his brother received, but that also meant that he had to remain at home rather than go to boarding school when the time came. Therefore, he had more than enough time to experience his aunts intensely. The female character in 'The Sex That Doesn't Shop' was, Munro admitted, a portrait of his Aunt Charlotte (always known as "Aunt Tom"). Aunts (and indeed most older women) are portrayed in Munro's fiction as cold, unimaginative, condescending and interfering, and this tallies with Ethel Munro's memoirs.

The children were eventually 'rescued' by the retirement of their father and his return to England. At the time, Hector was 16. After finishing his education and accompanying his family on several extended trips through Europe, he first followed his father's career path and then ventured into writing. His early successes in this field, described above, led him into journalism and into employment as a foreign correspondent for *The Morning Post*. He reported from the Balkans, Warsaw, Russia, and Paris, advancing from an anonymous source, paid only when his reports were printed, to a special correspondent whose stories appeared under his name and were protected by copyright. It was an eventful period. When Munro was in the Balkans, which had a justified reputation as the "powder keg of Europe",[5] the King and Queen of Serbia were murdered by revolutionaries, and he was an eye-witness to the bloody suppression of protests in St. Petersburg in 1905. His first-hand experiences of these countries helps explains the frequency with which Central Europe and Russia locations are used in his stories, even if it only be to provide a joke such as that in 'The Lost Sanjak'. But more than that, these borderlands of Europe seemed to provide Munro's imagination with the wildness and wildernesses that it was aways seeking out and which it connected with violence and vendettas. It was a world away from the refined society of Reginald and yet it is Munro's somewhat unnerving achievement that the two do not appear incongruous.

---

[5] The phrase is attributed to German Chancellor Otto von Bismarck.

Chronology

18 Dec. 1870	Hector Hugh Munro is born in Akyab, Burma, third child of Mary Frances Mercer and Charles Augustus Munro, inspector-general of police.
1872	Mother dies in a freak accident; Munro and his brother and sister sent to live with their grandmother and aunts in England.
1882	Munro sent to board at Pencarwick School, Exmouth.
1885	Starts Bedford Grammar School.
1887–93	Munro's father retires and returns permanently from Burma; takes family on extended trips through Europe.
1893	Munro goes to Burma to work in the colonial police force.
1894	Returns to London on grounds of ill health.
1899	'Dogged', Munro's first published short story, appears in *St. Paul's Magazine*, credited to "H.H.M.".
1900	Publication of *The Rise of the Russian Empire*, the fruit of several years' research in the British Library.

	Munro's first political sketches are published in the *Westminister Gazette*.
1902	*The Not So Stories* (political sketches) are published in *The Westminster Annual*.
	Publication of *The Westminster Alice* (political sketches with illustrations by F. Carruthers Gould).
1902–1908	Employed as foreign correspondent by *The Morning Post* in the Balkans, Warsaw, Russia, and Paris.
1904	Publication of *Reginald* (short stories).
1908	Returns to London.
1910	Publication of *Reginald in Russia* (short stories).
1911	Publication of *The Chronicles of Clovis* (short stories).
1912	Publication of *The Unbearable Bassington* (novel).
1913	Publication of *When William Came* (novel).
1914	Publication of *Beasts and Super-Beasts* (short stories).
	Death of father.
25 Aug. 1914	Enlists as a trooper in 2nd King Edward's Horse.
Sept. 1914	Transfers to 22nd Battalion, Royal Fusiliers.
Nov. 1915	Battalion is sent to France.
16 Nov. 1916	Shot by a German sniper near Beaumont Hamel in northern France. His last words had been "Put that bloody cigarette out!"

1919	Publication of *The Toys of Peace* (posthumously collected short stories).
1924	Publication of *The Square Egg and Other Sketches* (posthumously collected short stories and sketches).
1924	Publication of *The Watched Pot* (play, written in 1914 with Charles Maude).
1926–27	Publication of *The Works of Saki* (8 volumes).
1930	Publication of *The Complete Short Stories of Saki*
	First performance of *The Watched Pot*.
1943	London première of *The Watched Pot*.

Suggestions for further reading

General reading

Hattersley, Roy, *The Edwardians* (London: Abacus, 2006).

Samuel Hynes, *The Edwardian Turn of Mind* (Princeton: Princeton Univ. Press, 1968).

Malcolm, David and Cheryl Alexander Malcolm, eds, *A Companion to the British and Irish Short Story* (Chicester: Wiley-Blackwell, 2009).

On Saki

Byrne, Sandie, *The Unbearable Saki: The Work of H. H. Munro.* (Oxford: Oxford Univ. Press, 2007).

Drake, Robert, 'Saki's Ironic Stories'. *Texas Studies in Literature and Language*, Vol. 5, No. 3 (Autumn 1963), pp. 374-388.

Gibson, Brian. *Reading Saki: The Fiction of H.H. Munro.* (Jefferson, North Carolina: McFarland & Co., 2014).

———, 'Murdering Adulthood: Lost Girls, Boy Soldiers, and Child Killers in Saki's Fiction', in *Childhood in Edwardian Fiction: Worlds Enough and Time*, ed. by Adrienne E. Gavin and Andrew F. Humphries. (Houndmills, UK: Palgrave Macmillan, 2009), 208-223.

Gillen, Charles H., *H. H. Munro (Saki)*. (New York: Twayne, 1969).

Langguth, A. J., *Saki: A Life of Hector Hugh Munro*. (New York: Simon and Schuster, 1981).

Maxey, Ruth, 'Children are Given us to Discourage Our Better Instincts: The Paradoxical Treatment of Children in Saki's Short Fiction'. *Journal of the Short Story in English*, vol. 45 (Autumn 2005), 1-12.

Munro, Ethel M., 'Biography of Saki'. In *The Square Egg and Other Sketches, with Three Plays*. (New York: Viking, 1929).

Reynolds, Rothay, 'A Memoir of H. H. Munro'. In *The Toys of Peace and other Papers*. (London: John Lane The Bodley Head, 1919).

Spears, George J., *The Satire of Saki*. (New York: Exposition Press, 1963).

Editor's note

In annotating, I have principally been concerned with elucidating references that in some way help a modern reader to understand the stories and with pointing out allusions that might otherwise have gone unnoticed. I am aware that in doing so I may have laid myself open at times to the charge of explaining a joke, but my attitude is that most readers would prefer this to not knowing there was a joke in the first place.

I have largely refrained from glossing words that can be found in a decent desktop dictionary. In the case of actual people I have usually given only basic information: full name, dates of birth and death, profession.

I have of course ignored my self-imposed rules whenever I felt it really necessary.

Yet ah, that Spring should vanish with the Rose!
That Youth's sweet-scented manuscript should close!
The Nightingale that in the branches sang,
Ah whence, and whither flown again, who knows!

* * *

Yon rising Moon that looks for us again—
How oft hereafter will she wax and wane;
How oft hereafter rising look for us
Through this same Garden—and for *one* in vain!

And when like her, oh Sákí, you shall pass
Among the Guests Star-scatter'd on the Grass,
And in your blissful errand reach the spot
Where I made One—turn down an empty Glass!

* * *

Perplext no more with Human or Divine,
To-morrow's tangle to the winds resign,
And lose your fingers in the tresses of
The Cypress-slender Minister of Wine.

So when that Angel of the Darker Drink,
At last shall find you by the river-brink,
And, offering his Cup, invite your Soul
Forth to your Lips to quaff—you shall not shrink.

> (Lines from *The Rubáiyát of Omar Khayyám* copied
> by H. H. Munro into his commonplace book)

Reginald (1904)

Reginald

I did it—I who should have known better. I persuaded Reginald to go to the McKillops' garden-party against his will.

We all make mistakes occasionally.

"They know you're here, and they'll think it so funny if you don't go. And I want particularly to be in with Mrs. McKillop just now."

"I know, you want one of her smoke Persian kittens as a prospective wife for Wumples—or a husband, is it?" (Reginald has a magnificent scorn for details, other than sartorial.) "And I am expected to undergo social martyrdom to suit the connubial exigencies—"

"Reginald! It's nothing of the kind, only I'm sure Mrs. McKillop would be pleased if I brought you. Young men of your brilliant attractions are rather at a premium at her garden-parties."

"Should be at a premium in heaven," remarked Reginald complacently.

"There will be very few of you there, if that is what you mean. But seriously, there won't be any great strain upon your powers of endurance; I promise you that you shan't have to play croquet, or talk to the Archdeacon's wife, or do anything that is likely to bring on physical prostration. You can just wear your sweetest clothes and moderately amiable expression, and eat chocolate-creams with the appetite of a *blasé* parrot. Nothing more is demanded of you."

Reginald shut his eyes. "There will be the exhaustingly up-to-date young women who will ask me if I have seen *San Toy*:[6] a less progressive grade who will yearn to hear about the Diamond Jubilee—the historic event, not the horse.[7] With a little encouragement, they will inquire if I saw the Allies march into

---

[6] *San Toy, or The Emperor's Own*: a very successful musical comedy set in China, which premiered in London in 1899.

[7] Racehorse owned by Edward, Prince of Wales, which won a number of races in the period 1899-1901. Queen Victoria had celebrated her diamond jubilee in 1897.

Paris.[8] Why are women so fond of raking up the past? They're as bad as tailors, who invariably remember what you owe them for a suit long after you've ceased to wear it."

"I'll order lunch for one o'clock; that will give you two and a half hours to dress in."

Reginald puckered his brow into a tortured frown, and I knew that my point was gained. He was debating what tie would go with which waistcoat.

Even then I had my misgivings.

* * *

During the drive to the McKillops' Reginald was possessed with a great peace, which was not wholly to be accounted for by the fact that he had inveigled his feet into shoes a size too small for them. I misgave more than ever, and having once launched Reginald on to the McKillops' lawn, I established him near a seductive dish of *marrons glacés*, and as far from the Archdeacon's wife as possible; as I drifted away to a diplomatic distance I heard with painful distinctness the eldest Mawkby girl asking him if he had seen *San Toy*.

It must have been ten minutes later, not more, and I had been having *quite* an enjoyable chat with my hostess, and had promised to lend her *The Eternal City*[9] and my recipe for rabbit mayonnaise, and was just about to offer a kind home for her third Persian kitten, when I perceived, out of the corner of my eye, that Reginald was not where I had left him, and that the *marrons glacés* were untasted. At the same moment I became aware that old Colonel Mendoza was essaying to tell his classic story of how he introduced golf into India, and that Reginald was in dangerous proximity. There are occasions when Reginald is caviare to the Colonel.[10]

"When I was at Poona in '76—"[11]

---

[8] Referring to the end of the Napoleonic Wars nearly a century earlier.

[9] Novel by the very popular Hall Caine, published in 1901. It is a highly moral love story set in Rome, and was praised by many clergymen.

[10] Punning on "caviare to the general" (from *Hamlet*, though in the play "general" refers the common people, not the military rank).

[11] Modern spelling "Pune" (since 1978); the British Indian Army had a large cantonment there.

"My dear Colonel," purred Reginald, "fancy admitting such a thing! Such a give-away for one's age! I wouldn't admit being on this planet in '76." (Reginald in his wildest lapses into veracity never admits to being more than twenty-two.)

The Colonel went to the colour of a fig that has attained great ripeness, and Reginald, ignoring my efforts to intercept him, glided away to another part of the lawn. I found him a few minutes later happily engaged in teaching the youngest Rampage boy the approved theory of mixing absinthe, within full earshot of his mother. Mrs. Rampage occupies a prominent place in local Temperance movements.

As soon as I had broken up this unpromising *tête-à-tête* and settled Reginald where he could watch the croquet players losing their tempers, I wandered off to find my hostess and renew the kitten negotiations at the point where they had been interrupted. I did not succeed in running her down at once, and eventually it was Mrs. McKillop who sought me out, and her conversation was not of kittens.

"Your cousin is discussing *Zaza*[12] with the Archdeacon's wife; at least, he is discussing, she is ordering her carriage."

She spoke in the dry, staccato tone of one who repeats a French exercise, and I knew that as far as Millie McKillop was concerned, Wumples was devoted to a lifelong celibacy.

"If you don't mind," I said hurriedly, "I think we'd like our carriage ordered too," and I made a forced march in the direction of the croquet-ground.

I found everyone talking nervously and feverishly of the weather and the war in South Africa,[13] except Reginald, who was reclining in a comfortable chair with the dreamy, far-away look that a volcano might wear just after it had desolated entire villages. The Archdeacon's wife was buttoning up her gloves with a concentrated deliberation that was fearful to behold. I

---

[12] A play by French playwrights Pierre Berton and Charles Simon about a prostitute who becomes a music hall entertainer and the mistress of a married man. It was adapted into English in 1898.

[13] The (Second) Boer War, October 1899 to May 1902. See introduction.

shall have to treble my subscription to her Cheerful Sunday Evenings Fund before I dare set foot in her house again.

At that particular moment the croquet players finished their game, which had been going on without a symptom of finality during the whole afternoon. Why, I ask, should it have stopped precisely when a counter-attraction was so necessary? Everyone seemed to drift towards the area of disturbance, of which the chairs of the Archdeacon's wife and Reginald formed the storm-centre. Conversation flagged, and there settled upon the company that expectant hush that precedes the dawn—when your neighbours don't happen to keep poultry.

"What did the Caspian Sea?" asked Reginald, with appalling suddenness.

There were symptoms of a stampede. The Archdeacon's wife looked at me. Kipling or someone has described somewhere the look a foundered camel gives when the caravan moves on and leaves it to its fate.[14] The peptonised reproach in the good lady's eyes brought the passage vividly to my mind.

I played my last card.

"Reginald, it's getting late, and a sea-mist is coming on." I knew that the elaborate curl over his right eyebrow was not guaranteed to survive a sea-mist.

* * *

"Never, never again, will I take you to a garden-party. Never ... You behaved abominably ... What did the Caspian see?"

A shade of genuine regret for misused opportunities passed over Reginald's face.

"After all," he said, "I believe an apricot tie would have gone better with the lilac waistcoat."

Reginald on Christmas Presents

I wish it to be distinctly understood (said Reginald) that I don't want a "George, Prince of Wales" Prayer-book[15] as a Christmas

---

[14] Rudyard Kipling's poem 'OONTS (Northern India Transport Train)'.

[15] An edition of the standard prayer book used in Anglican churches was published to mark the investiture of the new Prince of Wales (the future George V)

REGINALD ON CHRISTMAS PRESENTS

present. The fact cannot be too widely known.

There ought (he continued) to be technical education classes on the science of present-giving. No one seems to have the faintest notion of what anyone else wants, and the prevalent ideas on the subject are not creditable to a civilised community.

There is, for instance, the female relative in the country who "knows a tie is always useful," and sends you some spotted horror that you could only wear in secret or in Tottenham Court Road.[16] It *might* have been useful had she kept it to tie up currant bushes with, when it would have served the double purpose of supporting the branches and frightening away the birds—for it is an admitted fact that the ordinary tomtit of commerce has a sounder aesthetic taste than the average female relative in the country.

Then there are aunts. They are always a difficult class to deal with in the matter of presents. The trouble is that one never catches them really young enough. By the time one has educated them to an appreciation of the fact that one does not wear red woollen mittens in the West End, they die, or quarrel with the family, or do something equally inconsiderate. That is why the supply of trained aunts is always so precarious.

There is my Aunt Agatha, *par exemple*, who sent me a pair of gloves last Christmas, and even got so far as to choose a kind that was being worn and had the correct number of buttons. But— *they were nines!*[17] I sent them to a boy whom I hated intimately: he didn't wear them, of course, but he could have—that was where the bitterness of death came in. It was nearly as consoling as sending white flowers to his funeral. Of course I wrote and told my aunt that they were the one thing that had been wanting to make existence blossom like a rose; I am afraid she thought

---

in 1901.

[16] Although not far from the fashionable parts of London, the Tottenham Court Road was a busy thoroughfare through a lower-class area, in which were located several large commercial establishments selling mass-produced clothing.

[17] Referring to the size, which would have made them quite large. Small hands were considered attractive, though this mostly applied to women.

me frivolous—she comes from the North, where they live in the fear of Heaven and the Earl of Durham.[18] (Reginald affects an exhaustive knowledge of things political, which furnishes an excellent excuse for not discussing them.) Aunts with a dash of foreign extraction in them are the most satisfactory in the way of understanding these things; but if you can't choose your aunt, it is wisest in the long-run to choose the present and send her the bill.

Even friends of one's own set, who might be expected to know better, have curious delusions on the subject. I am *not* collecting copies of the cheaper editions of Omar Khayyám.[19] I gave the last four that I received to the lift-boy, and I like to think of him reading them, with FitzGerald's notes,[20] to his aged mother. Lift-boys always have aged mothers; shows such nice feeling on their part, I think.

Personally, I can't see where the difficulty in choosing suitable presents lies. No boy who had brought himself up properly could fail to appreciate one of those decorative bottles of liqueurs that are so reverently staged in Morel's window[21]—and it wouldn't in the least matter if one did get duplicates. And there would always be the supreme moment of dreadful uncertainty whether it was *crême de menthe* or Chartreuse—like the expectant thrill on seeing your partner's hand turned up at bridge. People may say what they like about the decay of Christianity; the religious system that produced green Chartreuse can never really die.

And then, of course, there are liqueur glasses, and crystallised fruits, and tapestry curtains, and heaps of other necessaries of life that make really sensible presents—not to speak of luxuries, such as having one's bills paid, or getting

---

[18] Who was also Lord-Lieutenant of County Durham and therefore a prominent and powerful local figure.

[19] See introduction.

[20] See previous note.

[21] After amalgamation in the 1880s, more properly known as "Messrs Morel Bros, Cobbett & Son Ltd, Importers & Purveyors of High Class Comestibles", in Piccadilly.

something quite sweet in the way of jewellery. Unlike the alleged Good Woman of the Bible,[22] I'm not above rubies. When found, by the way, she must have been rather a problem at Christmas-time; nothing short of a blank cheque would have fitted the situation. Perhaps it's as well that she's died out.

The great charm about me (concluded Reginald) is that I am so easily pleased.

But I draw the line at a "Prince of Wales" Prayer-book.

Reginald on the Academy

"One goes to the Academy[23] in self-defence," said Reginald. "It is the one topic one has in common with the Country Cousins."

"It is almost a religious observance with them," said the Other. "A kind of artistic Mecca, and when the good ones die they go—"

"To the Chantrey Bequest.[24] The mystery is *what* they find to talk about in the country."

"There are two subjects of conversation in the country: Servants, and Can fowls be made to pay? The first, I believe, is compulsory, the second optional."

"As a function," resumed Reginald, "the Academy is a failure."

"You think it would be tolerable without the pictures?"

"The pictures are all right, in their way; after all, one can always *look* at them if one is bored with one's surroundings, or wants to avoid an imminent acquaintance."

---

[22] "Who can find a virtuous woman? for her price is far above rubies" (Proverbs 31:10).

[23] The Royal Academy of Arts on Piccadilly in London. Its May exhibition marked the beginning of the London social season.

[24] The English sculptor Sir Francis Leggatt Chantrey (7 April 1781–25 November 1841) left his entire personal fortune to the Royal Academy for the purchase of British sculptures and paintings. The resulting collection was put on display in the National Gallery of British Art in London (today known as Tate Britain). At the time this story was written, the trustees' purchasing policy had been sharply criticised for being unadventurous and favouring fellow Royal Academicians.

"Even that doesn't always save one. There is the inevitable female whom you met once in Devonshire, or the Matoppo Hills,[25] or somewhere, who charges up to you with the remark that it's funny how one always meets people one knows at the Academy. Personally, I *don't* think it funny."

"I suffered in that way just now," said Reginald plaintively, "from a woman whose word I had to take that she had met me last summer in Brittany."

"I hope you were not too brutal?"

"I merely told her with engaging simplicity that the art of life was the avoidance of the unattainable."

"Did she try and work it out on the back of her catalogue?"

"Not there and then. She murmured something about being 'so clever.' Fancy coming to the Academy to be clever!"

"To be clever in the afternoon argues that one is dining nowhere in the evening."

"Which reminds me that I can't remember whether I accepted an invitation from you to dine at Kettner's[26] to-night."

"On the other hand, I can remember with startling distinctness not having asked you to."

"So much certainty is unbecoming in the young; so we'll consider that settled. What were you talking about? Oh, pictures. Personally, I rather like them; they are so refreshingly real and probable, they take one away from the unrealities of life."

"One likes to escape from oneself occasionally."

"That is the disadvantage of a portrait; as a rule, one's bitterest friends can find nothing more to ask than the faithful unlikeness that goes down to posterity as oneself. I hate posterity—it's so fond of having the last word. Of course, as regards portraits, there are exceptions."

"For instance?"

"To die before being painted by Sargent[27] is to go to heaven prematurely."

---

[25] In what is today Zimbabwe (formerly Rhodesia).

[26] A restaurant in Soho, first opened in 1867 and popular with people such as Oscar Wilde and Edward VII.

[27] John Singer Sargent (1856-1925).

"With the necessary care and impatience, you may avoid that catastrophe."

"If you're going to be rude," said Reginald, "I shall dine with you to-morrow night as well. The chief vice of the Academy," he continued, "is its nomenclature. Why, for instance, should an obvious trout-stream with a palpable rabbit sitting in the foreground be called 'an evening dream of unbeclouded peace,' or something of that sort?"

"You think," said the Other, "that a name should economise description rather than stimulate imagination?"

"Properly chosen, it should do both. There is my lady kitten at home, for instance; I've called it Derry."[28]

"Suggests nothing to my imagination but protracted sieges and religious animosities. Of course, I don't know your kitten—"

"Oh, you're silly. It's a sweet name, and it answers to it—when it wants to. Then, if there are any unseemly noises in the night, they can be explained succinctly: Derry and Toms."[29]

"You might almost charge for the advertisement. But as applied to pictures, don't you think your system would be too subtle, say, for the Country Cousins?"

"Every reformation must have its victims. You can't expect the fatted calf to share the enthusiasm of the angels over the prodigal's return.[30] Another darling weakness of the Academy is that none of its luminaries must 'arrive' in a hurry. You can see them coming for years, like a Balkan trouble or a street improvement, and by the time they have painted a thousand or so square yards of canvas, their work begins to be recognised."

---

[28] Referring to the city of (London)derry in the north of Ireland, famous in Irish Protestant folk memory for withstanding the besieging army of the Catholic monarch James II during the war of the Glorious Revolution (1688-1689).

[29] A department store for the upper class on Kensington High Street, founded 1862.

[30] See Luke 15:11-32.

"Someone who Must Not be Contradicted said that a man must be a success by the time he's thirty, or never."[31]

"To have reached thirty," said Reginald, "is to have failed in life."

Reginald at the Theatre

"After all," said the Duchess vaguely, "there are certain things you can't get away from. Right and wrong, good conduct and moral rectitude, have certain well-defined limits."

"So, for the matter of that," replied Reginald, "has the Russian Empire. The trouble is that the limits are not always in the same place."

Reginald and the Duchess regarded each other with mutual distrust, tempered by a scientific interest. Reginald considered that the Duchess had much to learn; in particular, not to hurry out of the Carlton[32] as though afraid of losing one's last 'bus. A woman, he said, who is careless of disappearances is capable of leaving town before Goodwood,[33] and dying at the wrong moment of an unfashionable disease.

The Duchess thought that Reginald did not exceed the ethical standard which circumstances demanded.

"Of course," she resumed combatively, "it's the prevailing fashion to believe in perpetual change and mutability, and all that sort of thing, and to say we are all merely an improved form of primeval ape—of course you subscribe to that doctrine?"

"I think it decidedly premature; in most people I know the process is far from complete."

---

[31] This is probably a coded reference to Oscar Wilde (mention of whose name was taboo at this time due to his conviction for homosexuality). It is not a direct quotation; the most likely source is Sir Robert Chiltern's comment in *An Ideal Husband* (1895) that "Youth is the time for success". Reginald's answer in the following line also echoes comments in this play and in other works by Wilde about lying to appear younger than one actually is.

[32] One of London's most fashionable hotels, opened in 1899. The kitchens were run by famed French chef Auguste Escoffier.

[33] The horse races at Goodwood near Chichester, West Sussex, held every year in July/August, are an important race meeting and high society social event.

REGINALD AT THE THEATRE 13

"And equally of course you are quite irreligious?"

"Oh, by no means. The fashion just now is a Roman Catholic frame of mind with an Agnostic conscience: you get the mediaeval picturesqueness of the one with the modern conveniences of the other."

The Duchess suppressed a sniff. She was one of those people who regard the Church of England with patronising affection, as if it were something that had grown up in their kitchen garden.

"But there are other things," she continued, "which I suppose are to a certain extent sacred even to you. Patriotism, for instance, and Empire, and Imperial responsibility, and blood-is-thicker-than-water, and all that sort of thing."

Reginald waited for a couple of minutes before replying, while the Lord of Rimini[34] temporarily monopolised the acoustic possibilities of the theatre.

"That is the worst of a tragedy," he observed, "one can't always hear oneself talk. Of course I accept the Imperial idea and the responsibility. After all, I would just as soon think in Continents as anywhere else. And some day, when the season is over and we have the time, you shall explain to me the exact blood-brotherhood and all that sort of thing that exists between a French Canadian and a mild Hindoo and a Yorkshireman, for instance."

"Oh, well, 'dominion over palm and pine,'[35] you know," quoted the Duchess hopefully; "of course we mustn't forget that we're all part of the great Anglo-Saxon Empire."

"Which for its part is rapidly becoming a suburb of Jerusalem.[36] A very pleasant suburb, I admit, and quite a charming Jerusalem. But still a suburb."

"Really, to be told one's living in a suburb when one is conscious of spreading the benefits of civilisation all over the world!

---

[34] Probably in Gabriele d'Annunzio's tragedy *Francesca da Rimini* (1901, translated into English by Arthur Symonds in 1902).

[35] From the poem 'Recessional' by Rudyard Kipling.

[36] In the last two decades there had been an influx of Jewish immigrants, mostly from Russia. The number in London roughly tripled over the two decades up to 1900.

Philanthropy—I suppose you will say *that* is a comfortable delusion; and yet even you must admit that whenever want or misery or starvation is known to exist, however distant or difficult of access, we instantly organise relief on the most generous scale, and distribute it, if need be, to the uttermost ends of the earth."

The Duchess paused, with a sense of ultimate triumph. She had made the same observation at a drawing-room meeting, and it had been extremely well received.

"I wonder," said Reginald, "if you have ever walked down the Embankment[37] on a winter night?"

"Gracious, no, child! Why do you ask?"

"I didn't; I only wondered. And even your philanthropy, practised in a world where everything is based on competition, must have a debit as well as a credit account. The young ravens cry for food."

"And are fed."

"Exactly. Which presupposes that something else is fed upon."

"Oh, you're simply exasperating. You've been reading Nietzsche[38] till you haven't got any sense of moral proportion left. May I ask if you are governed by *any* laws of conduct whatever?"

"There are certain fixed rules that one observes for one's own comfort. For instance, never be flippantly rude to any inoffensive grey-bearded stranger that you may meet in pine forests or hotel smoking-rooms on the Continent. It always turns out to be the King of Sweden."[39]

"The restraint must be dreadfully irksome to you. When I was younger, boys of your age used to be nice and innocent."

"Now we are only nice. One must specialise in these days. Which reminds me of the man I read of in some sacred book

---

[37] The Thames Embankment. Its seats and arches meant it filled at night with London's homeless looking for somewhere to sleep.

[38] German philosopher (1844-1900) whose works vehemently rejected Christianity and conventional notions of morality.

[39] Oskar II (1829-1907), who was renowned for his fairness and independence from politics. He enjoyed travelling through Europe, often combining his recreation with soft diplomacy.

who was given a choice of what he most desired. And because he didn't ask for titles and honours and dignities, but only for immense wealth, these other things came to him also."

"I am sure you didn't read about him in any sacred book."

"Yes; I fancy you will find him in Debrett."[40]

Reginald's Peace Poem

"I'm writing a poem on Peace,"[41] said Reginald, emerging from a sweeping operation through a tin of mixed biscuits, in whose depths a macaroon or two might yet be lurking.

"Something of the kind seems to have been attempted already," said the Other.

"Oh, I know; but I may never have the chance again. Besides, I've got a new fountain pen. I don't pretend to have gone on any very original lines; in writing about Peace the thing is to say what everybody else is saying, only to say it better. It begins with the usual ornithological emotion:

> 'When the widgeon westward winging
> Heard the folk Vereeniginging,[42]
> Heard the shouting and the singing—'"

"Vereeniginging is good, but why widgeon?"

"Why not? Anything that winged westward would naturally begin with a *w*."

"Need it wing westward?"

"The bird must go somewhere. You wouldn't have it hang around and look foolish. Then I've brought in something about the heedless hartebeest[43] galloping over the deserted veldt."

---

[40] Debrett's *The Peerage of England, Scotland, and Ireland*, was, and is, the standard guide to the British nobility.

[41] The recently concluded Boer War. See introduction.

[42] Vereeniging is a city in South Africa. At the time it was part of the Transvaal province. The city's name derives from the Dutch for "union". The Treaty of Vereeniging ended the Second Boer War.

[43] A type of large antelope.

"Of course you know it's practically extinct in those regions?"

"I can't help *that*, it gallops so nicely. I make it have all sorts of unexpected yearnings:

> 'Mother, may I go and maffick,[44]
> Tear around and hinder traffic?'

Of course you'll say there would be no traffic worth bothering about on the bare and sun-scorched veldt, but there's no other word that rhymes with maffick."

"Seraphic?"

Reginald considered. "It might do, but I've got a lot about angels later on. You must have angels in a Peace poem; I know dreadfully little about their habits."

"They can do unexpected things, like the hartebeest."

"Of course. Then I turn on London, the City of Dreadful Nocturnes,[45] resonant with hymns of joy and thanksgiving:

> 'And the sleeper, eye unlidding,
> Heard a voice for ever bidding
> Much farewell to Dolly Gray;[46]
> Turning weary on his truckle-
> Bed he heard the honey-suckle
> Lauded in apiarian lay.'

---

[44] The town of Mefeking held out against a siege by the Boers for 215 days (1899–1900). News of its relief was greeted in Britain with such joy that it led to the coinage of a short-lived verbal noun 'mafficking', meaning 'celebrating loudly and extravagantly'.

[45] Punning on the title of Scottish poet James Thomson's long poem *The City of Dreadful Night* (1874). "Nocturnes" probably refers here not to musical pieces but to the paintings of night-time London by James Abbott McNeill Whistler (1834-1903), which attracted a great deal of criticism at the time.

[46] "Goodbye Dolly Gray" was a song written by Will D. Cobb (lyrics) and Paul Barnes (music), ventriloquising the feelings of a soldier going off to war. It was popular in the USA during the Spanish-American War of 1898 and (after a few changes to the lyrics) in the UK during the Boer War.

Longfellow[47] at his best wrote nothing like that."

"I agree with you."

"I wish you wouldn't. I've a sweet temper, but I can't stand being agreed with. And I'm so worried about the aasvogel."[48]

Reginald stared dismally at the biscuit-tin, which now presented an unattractive array of rejected cracknels.

"I believe," he murmured, "if I could find a woman with an unsatisfied craving for cracknels, I should marry her."

"What is the tragedy of the aasvogel?" asked the Other sympathetically.

"Oh, simply that there's no rhyme for it. I thought about it all the time I was dressing—it's dreadfully bad for one to think whilst one's dressing—and all lunch-time, and I'm still hung up over it. I feel like those unfortunate automobilists who achieve an unenviable notoriety by coming to a hopeless stop with their cars in the most crowded thoroughfares. I'm afraid I shall have to drop the aasvogel, and it did give such lovely local colour to the thing."

"Still you've got the heedless hartebeest."

"And quite a decorative bit of moral admonition—when you've worried the meaning out:

'Cease, War, thy bubbling madness that the wine shares,
And bid thy legions turn their swords to mine shares.'

Mine shares seems to fit the case better than ploughshares.[49] There's lots more about the blessings of Peace, shall I go on reading it?"

"If I must make a choice, I think I would rather they went on with the war."

---

[47] Henry Wadsworth Longfellow (1807-1882).

[48] Literally, 'carrion bird': a vulture.

[49] A reference to "they shall beat their swords into plowshares" in Isaiah 2:3-4; control of the Transvaal and the Orange Free State brought with it the right to exploit their mineral riches, such as their gold and diamond mines.

Reginald's Choir Treat

"Never," wrote Reginald to his most darling friend, "be a pioneer. It's the Early Christian that gets the fattest lion."

Reginald, in his way, was a pioneer.

None of the rest of his family had anything approaching Titian hair or a sense of humour, and they used primroses as a table decoration.

It follows that they never understood Reginald, who came down late to breakfast, and nibbled toast, and said disrespectful things about the universe. The family ate porridge, and believed in everything, even the weather forecast.

Therefore the family was relieved when the vicar's daughter undertook the reformation of Reginald. Her name was Amabel; it was the vicar's one extravagance.[50] Amabel was accounted a beauty and intellectually gifted; she never played tennis, and was reputed to have read Maeterlinck's *Life of the Bee*.[51] If you abstain from tennis *and* read Maeterlinck in a small country village, you are of necessity intellectual. Also she had been twice to Fécamp[52] to pick up a good French accent from the Americans staying there; consequently she had a knowledge of the world which might be considered useful in dealings with a worldling.

Hence the congratulations in the family when Amabel undertook the reformation of its wayward member.

Amabel commenced operations by asking her unsuspecting pupil to tea in the vicarage garden; she believed in the healthy influence of natural surroundings, never having been in Sicily, where things are different.

And like every woman who has ever preached repentance to unregenerate youth, she dwelt on the sin of an empty life, which always seems so much more scandalous in the country, where

---

[50] The name had not been common since the Middle Ages, although it had a brief revival in the nineteenth century as part of the Victorian fascination with the medieval.

[51] Maurice Maeterlinck, symbolist writer (1862-1949). His *Life of the Bee* was the first of his very successful popular science books.

[52] Seaside resort on the coast of Normandy.

people rise early to see if a new strawberry has happened during the night.

Reginald recalled the lilies of the field, "which simply sat and looked beautiful, and defied competition."[53]

"But that is not an example for us to follow," gasped Amabel.

"Unfortunately, we can't afford to. You don't know what a world of trouble I take in trying to rival the lilies in their artistic simplicity."

"You are really indecently vain of your appearance. A good life is infinitely preferable to good looks."

"You agree with me that the two are incompatible. I always say beauty is only sin deep."

Amabel began to realise that the battle is not always to the strong-minded.[54] With the immemorial resource of her sex, she abandoned the frontal attack, and laid stress on her unassisted labours in parish work, her mental loneliness, her discouragements—and at the right moment she produced strawberries and cream. Reginald was obviously affected by the latter, and when his preceptress suggested that he might begin the strenuous life[55] by helping her to supervise the annual outing of the bucolic infants who composed the local choir, his eyes shone with the dangerous enthusiasm of a convert.

Reginald entered on the strenuous life alone, as far as Amabel was concerned. The most virtuous women are not proof against damp grass, and Amabel kept her bed with a cold. Reginald called it a dispensation; it had been the dream of his

---

[53] Reginald's theologically suspect understanding of Matthew 6:28-29. (See also Luke 12:27.)

[54] Another religious allusion, this time to Ecclesiastes 9:11: "Again I saw that under the sun the race is not to the swift, nor the battle to the strong, nor bread to the wise, nor riches to the intelligent, nor favor to those with knowledge, but time and chance happen to them all."

[55] 'The Strenuous Life' was the title of a speech made by US President Theodore Roosevelt in 1899, setting out his personal credo. It begins: "I wish to preach, not the doctrine of ignoble ease, but the doctrine of the strenuous life, the life of toil and effort, of labor and strife; to preach that highest form of success which comes, not to the man who desires mere easy peace, but to the man who does not shrink from danger, from hardship, or from bitter toil, and who out of these wins the splendid ultimate triumph."

life to stage-manage a choir outing. With strategic insight, he led his shy, bullet-headed charges to the nearest woodland stream and allowed them to bathe; then he seated himself on their discarded garments and discoursed on their immediate future, which, he decreed, was to embrace a Bacchanalian procession through the village. Forethought had provided the occasion with a supply of tin whistles, but the introduction of a he-goat from a neighbouring orchard was a brilliant afterthought. Properly, Reginald explained, there should have been an outfit of panther skins; as it was, those who had spotted handkerchiefs were allowed to wear them, which they did with thankfulness. Reginald recognised the impossibility, in the time at his disposal, of teaching his shivering neophytes a chant in honour of Bacchus,[56] so he started them off with a more familiar, if less appropriate, temperance hymn. After all, he said, it is the spirit of the thing that counts. Following the etiquette of dramatic authors on first nights, he remained discreetly in the background while the procession, with extreme diffidence and the goat, wound its way lugubriously towards the village. The singing had died down long before the main street was reached, but the miserable wailing of pipes brought the inhabitants to their doors. Reginald said he had seen something like it in pictures; the villagers had seen nothing like it in their lives, and remarked as much freely.

Reginald's family never forgave him. They had no sense of humour.

Reginald on Worries

I have (said Reginald) an aunt who worries. She's not really an aunt—a sort of amateur one, and they aren't really worries. She is a social success, and has no domestic tragedies worth speaking of, so she adopts any decorative sorrows that are going, myself included. In that way she's the antithesis, or whatever you call it, to those sweet, uncomplaining women

---

[56]The Roman god of wine, ritual madness and divine ecstasy.

one knows who have seen trouble, and worn blinkers ever since. Of course, one just loves them for it, but I must confess they make me uncomfy; they remind one so of a duck that goes flapping about with forced cheerfulness long after its head's been cut off. Ducks have *no* repose. Now, my aunt has a shade of hair that suits her, and a cook who quarrels with the other servants, which is always a hopeful sign, and a conscience that's absentee for about eleven months of the year, and only turns up at Lent to annoy her husband's people, who are considerably Lower[57] than the angels, so to speak: with all these natural advantages—she says her particular tint of bronze is a natural advantage, and there can be no two opinions as to the advantage—of course she has to send out for her afflictions, like those restaurants where they haven't got a licence.[58] The system has this advantage, that you can fit your unhappinesses in with your other engagements, whereas real worries have a way of arriving at meal-times, and when you're dressing, or other solemn moments. I knew a canary once that had been trying for months and years to hatch out a family, and everyone looked upon it as a blameless infatuation, like the sale of Delagoa Bay,[59] which would be an annual loss to the Press agencies if it ever came to pass; and one day the bird really did bring it off, in the middle of family prayers. I say the middle, but it was also the end: you can't go on being thankful for daily bread when you are wondering what on earth very new canaries expect to be fed on.

At present she's rather in a Balkan state of mind about the treatment of the Jews in Roumania. Personally, I think the Jews have estimable qualities; they're so kind to their poor—and

---

[57] "Lower" here means belonging to the "Low Church" tendency in the Church of England, which is more evangelical and has more in common with other Protestant dissenting churches than the "High Church", which is closer in terms of ritual and doctrine to the Roman Catholic Church.

[58] To sell alcohol on the premises.

[59] There had been a long-running dispute between the UK and Portugal over this bay, now called Maputo Bay, on the coast of Mozambique, and over trading rights in the surrounding area. Another dispute began in 1889 over the railway running from the bay to the Transvaal. It was finally settled in 1900.

to our rich. I daresay in Roumania the cost of living beyond one's income isn't so great. Over here the trouble is that so many people who have money to throw about seem to have such vague ideas where to throw it. That fund, for instance, to relieve the victims of sudden disasters—what is a sudden disaster? There's Marion Mulciber, who *would* think she could play bridge, just as she would think she could ride down a hill on a bicycle; on that occasion she went to a hospital, now she's gone into a Sisterhood—lost all she had, you know, and gave the rest to Heaven. Still, you can't call it a sudden calamity; *that* occurred when poor dear Marion was born. The doctors said at the time that she couldn't live more than a fortnight, and she's been trying ever since to see if she could. Women are so opinionated.

And then there's the Education Question—not that I can see that there's anything to worry about in that direction. To my mind, education is an absurdly over-rated affair. At least, one never took it very seriously at school, where everything was done to bring it prominently under one's notice. Anything that is worth knowing one practically teaches oneself, and the rest obtrudes itself sooner or later. The reason one's elders know so comparatively little is because they have to unlearn so much that they acquired by way of education before we were born. Of course I'm a believer in Nature-study; as I said to Lady Beauwhistle, if you want a lesson in elaborate artificiality, just watch the studied unconcern of a Persian cat entering a crowded salon, and then go and practise it for a fortnight. The Beauwhistles weren't born in the Purple,[60] you know, but they're getting there on the instalment system—so much down, and the rest when you feel like it. They have kind hearts, and they never forget birthdays. I forget what he was, something in the City, where the patriotism comes from; and she—oh, well, her frocks are built in Paris, but she wears them with a strong English accent. So public-spirited of her. I think she must have been very strictly brought up, she's so desperately anxious to do

---
[60]The aristocracy.

the wrong thing correctly. Not that it really matters nowadays, as I told her: I know some perfectly virtuous people who are received everywhere.

Reginald on House-Parties

The drawback is, one never really *knows* one's hosts and hostesses. One gets to know their fox-terriers and their chrysanthemums, and whether the story about the go-cart can be turned loose in the drawing-room, or must be told privately to each member of the party, for fear of shocking public opinion; but one's host and hostess are a sort of human hinterland that one never has the time to explore.

There was a fellow I stayed with once in Warwickshire who farmed his own land, but was otherwise quite steady. Should never have suspected him of having a soul, yet not very long afterwards he eloped with a lion-tamer's widow and set up as a golf-instructor somewhere on the Persian Gulf; dreadfully immoral, of course, because he was only an indifferent player, but still, it showed imagination. His wife was really to be pitied, because he had been the only person in the house who understood how to manage the cook's temper, and now she has to put "D.V."[61] on her dinner invitations. Still, that's better than a domestic scandal; a woman who leaves her cook never wholly recovers her position in Society.

I suppose the same thing holds good with the hosts; they seldom have more than a superficial acquaintance with their guests, and so often just when they do get to know you a bit better, they leave off knowing you altogether. There was *rather* a breath of winter in the air when I left those

Dorsetshire people. You see, they had asked me down to shoot, and I'm not particularly immense[62] at that sort of thing. There's such a deadly sameness about partridges; when you've

---

[61] Latin: *Deo volente* (God willing).
[62] Slang for "excellent".

missed one, you've missed the lot—at least, that's been my experience. And they tried to rag me in the smoking-room about not being able to hit a bird at five yards, a sort of bovine ragging that suggested cows buzzing round a gadfly and thinking they were teasing it. So I got up the next morning at early dawn—I know it was dawn, because there were lark-noises in the sky, and the grass looked as if it had been left out all night—and hunted up the most conspicuous thing in the bird line that I could find, and measured the distance, as nearly as it would let me, and shot away all I knew. They said afterwards that it was a tame bird; that's simply *silly*, because it was awfully wild at the first few shots. Afterwards it quieted down a bit, and when its legs had stopped waving farewells to the landscape I got a gardener-boy to drag it into the hall, where everybody must see it on their way to the breakfast-room. I breakfasted upstairs myself. I gathered afterwards that the meal was tinged with a very unchristian spirit. I suppose it's unlucky to bring peacock's feathers into a house;[63]: anyway, there was a blue-pencilly[64] look in my hostess's eye when I took my departure.

Some hostesses, of course, will forgive anything, even unto pavonicide (is there such a word?), as long as one is nice-looking and sufficiently unusual to counterbalance some of the others; and there *are* others—the girl, for instance, who reads Meredith,[65] and appears at meals with unnatural punctuality in a frock that's made at home and repented at leisure. She eventually finds her way to India and gets married, and comes home to admire the Royal Academy,[66] and to imagine that an indifferent prawn curry is for ever an effective substitute for all that we have been taught to believe is luncheon. It's then that she is really dangerous; but at her worst she is never quite so bad as the

---

[63] According to superstition it is bad luck to have peacock feathers inside a house.
[64] Censorious.
[65] George Meredith, novelist and poet (1828-1909).
[66] See note 23.

woman who fires *Exchange and Mart* questions[67] at you without the least provocation. Imagine the other day, just when I was doing my best to understand half the things I was saying, being asked by one of those seekers after country home truths how many fowls she could keep in a run ten feet by six, or whatever it was! I told her whole crowds, as long as she kept the door shut, and the idea didn't seem to have struck her before; at least, she brooded over it for the rest of dinner.

Of course, as I say, one never really *knows* one's ground, and one may make mistakes occasionally. But then one's mistakes sometimes turn out assets in the long-run: if we had never bungled away our American colonies we might never have had the boy from the States to teach us how to wear our hair and cut our clothes, and we must get our ideas from somewhere, I suppose. Even the Hooligan[68] was probably invented in China centuries before we thought of him. England must wake up, as the Duke of Devonshire said the other day, wasn't it?[69] Oh, well, it was someone else. Not that I ever indulge in despair about the Future; there always have been men who have gone about despairing of the Future, and when the Future arrives it says nice, superior things about their having acted according to their lights. It is dreadful to think that other people's grandchildren may one day rise up and call one amiable.

There are moments when one sympathises with Herod.

Reginald at the Carlton[70]

"A most variable climate," said the Duchess; "and how unfortunate that we should have had that very cold weather at a time when coal was so dear! So distressing for the poor."

---

[67]The paper *Exchange and Mart* had been launched in 1868 to put buyers and sellers in direct contact with each other. Reginald is presumably using it to mean "lower-class and utilitarian".

[68]At the time, this word was a new coinage. (First attested in 1898.)

[69]It was the Prince of Wales, and what he actually said was "England must wake up commercially". He was speaking at a conference at the Guildhall in 1901.

[70]See note 32.

"Someone has observed that Providence is always on the side of the big dividends," remarked Reginald.

The Duchess ate an anchovy in a shocked manner; she was sufficiently old-fashioned to dislike irreverence towards dividends.

Reginald had left the selection of a feeding-ground to her womanly intuition, but he chose the wine himself, knowing that womanly intuition stops short at claret. A woman will cheerfully choose husbands for her less attractive friends, or take sides in a political controversy without the least knowledge of the issues involved—but no woman ever cheerfully chose a claret.

"Hors d'œuvres have always a pathetic interest for me," said Reginald: "they remind me of one's childhood that one goes through, wondering what the next course is going to be like—and during the rest of the menu one wishes one had eaten more of the hors d'oeuvres. Don't you love watching the different ways people have of entering a restaurant? There is the woman who races in as though her whole scheme of life were held together by a one-pin despotism which might abdicate its functions at any moment; it's really a relief to see her reach her chair in safety. Then there are the people who troop in with an-unpleasant-duty-to-perform air, as if they were angels of Death entering a plague city. You see that type of Briton very much in hotels abroad. And nowadays there are always the Johannes-bourgeois, who bring a Cape-to-Cairo[71] atmosphere with them—what may be called the Rand Manner, I suppose."[72]

"Talking about hotels abroad," said the Duchess, "I am preparing notes for a lecture at the Club on the educational effects of modern travel, dealing chiefly with the moral side of the question. I was talking to Lady Beauwhistle's aunt the other day—she's just come back from Paris, you know. Such a sweet woman—"

---

[71] Atmosphere of Britain's African colonies (which very nearly reached from Cairo to the South African Cape).

[72] Punning on the place names Johannesburg and Witwatersrand (often shortened to "the Rand").

REGINALD AT THE CARLTON

"And so silly. In these days of the over-education of women she's quite refreshing. They say some people went through the siege of Paris without knowing that France and Germany were at war; but the Beauwhistle aunt is credited with having passed the whole winter in Paris under the impression that the Humberts[73] were a kind of bicycle ...Isn't there a bishop or somebody who believes we shall meet all the animals we have known on earth in another world? How frightfully embarrassing to meet a whole shoal of whitebait you had last known at Prince's![74] I'm sure in my nervousness I should talk of nothing but lemons. Still, I daresay they would be quite as offended if one hadn't eaten them. I know if I were served up at a cannibal feast I should be dreadfully annoyed if anyone found fault with me for not being tender enough, or having been kept too long."

"My idea about the lecture," resumed the Duchess hurriedly, "is to inquire whether promiscuous Continental travel doesn't tend to weaken the moral fibre of the social conscience. There are people one knows, quite nice people when they are in England, who are so *different* when they are anywhere the other side of the Channel."

"The people with what I call Tauchnitz morals,"[75] observed Reginald. "On the whole, I think they get the best of two very desirable worlds. And, after all, they charge so much for excess luggage on some of those foreign lines that it's really an economy to leave one's reputation behind one occasionally."

"A scandal, my dear Reginald, is as much to be avoided at Monaco or any of those places as at Exeter, let us say."

---

[73]The Humberts were a husband and wife who perpetrated a twenty-year long fraud in France, taking out huge loans on the back of a claimed inheritance from an American millionaire. The deception was finally uncovered in 1902. The Humberts had already fled to Madrid but were caught and sentenced to imprisonment with hard labour. Reginald is making a play on the name a high-class British bicycle manufacturing company called Humber.

[74]The Prince's Hall was a restaurant and venue for concerts and balls on Piccadilly.

[75]Tauchnitz was the name of a German publishing company that printed English-language editions of British writers for sale in mainland Europe. The books carried the warning "Not to be introduced into England or into any British colony".

"Scandal, my dear Irene—I may call you Irene, mayn't I?"

"I don't know that you have known me long enough for that."

"I've known you longer than your god-parents had when they took the liberty of calling you that name. Scandal is merely the compassionate allowance which the gay make to the humdrum. Think how many blameless lives are brightened by the blazing indiscretions of other people. Tell me, who is the woman with the old lace at the table on our left? Oh, *that* doesn't matter; it's quite the thing nowadays to stare at people as if they were yearlings at Tattersall's."[76]

"Mrs. Spelvexit? Quite a charming woman; separated from her husband—"

"Incompatibility of income?"

"Oh, nothing of that sort. By miles of frozen ocean, I was going to say. He explores ice-floes and studies the movements of herrings, and has written a most interesting book on the home-life of the Esquimaux; but naturally he has very little home-life of his own."

"A husband who comes home with the Gulf Stream *would* be rather a tied-up asset."

"His wife is exceedingly sensible about it. She collects postage-stamps. Such a resource. Those people with her are the Whimples, very old acquaintances of mine; they're always having trouble, poor things."

"Trouble is not one of those fancies you can take up and drop at any moment; it's like a grouse-moor or the opium-habit—once you start it you've got to keep it up."

"Their eldest son was such a disappointment to them; they wanted him to be a linguist, and spent no end of money on having him taught to speak—oh, dozens of languages!—and then he became a Trappist monk. And the youngest, who was intended for the American marriage market,[77] has developed political tendencies, and writes pamphlets about the housing of the

---

[76] The main race horse auctioneers in the UK.

[77] The marriage of noble but impoverished Britons with rich, socially ambitious Americans was a relatively common phenomenon of the period.

poor. Of course it's a most important question, and I devote a good deal of time to it myself in the mornings; but, as Laura Whimple says, it's as well to have an establishment of one's own before agitating about other people's. She feels it very keenly, but she always maintains a cheerful appetite, which I think is so unselfish of her."

"There are different ways of taking disappointment. There was a girl I knew who nursed a wealthy uncle through a long illness, borne by her with Christian fortitude, and then he died and left his money to a swine-fever hospital. She found she'd about cleared stock in fortitude by that time, and now she gives drawing-room recitations. That's what I call being vindictive."

"Life is full of its disappointments," observed the Duchess, "and I suppose the art of being happy is to disguise them as illusions. But that, my dear Reginald, becomes more difficult as one grows older."

"I think it's more generally practised than you imagine. The young have aspirations that never come to pass, the old have reminiscences of what never happened. It's only the middle-aged who are really conscious of their limitations—that is why one should be so patient with them. But one never is."

"After all," said the Duchess, "the disillusions of life may depend on our way of assessing it. In the minds of those who come after us we may be remembered for qualities and successes which we quite left out of the reckoning."

"It's not always safe to depend on the commemorative tendencies of those who come after us. There may have been disillusionments in the lives of the mediæval saints, but they would scarcely have been better pleased if they could have foreseen that their names would be associated nowadays chiefly with racehorses and the cheaper clarets. And now, if you can tear yourself away from the salted almonds, we'll go and have coffee under the palms that are so necessary for our discomfort."

Reginald on Besetting Sins

THE WOMAN WHO TOLD THE TRUTH

There was once (said Reginald) a woman who told the truth. Not all at once, of course, but the habit grew upon her gradually, like lichen on an apparently healthy tree. She had no children—otherwise it might have been different. It began with little things, for no particular reason except that her life was a rather empty one, and it is so easy to slip into the habit of telling the truth in little matters. And then it became difficult to draw the line at more important things, until at last she took to telling the truth about her age; she said she was forty-two and five months—by that time, you see, she was veracious even to months. It may have been pleasing to the angels, but her elder sister was not gratified. On the Woman's birthday, instead of the opera-tickets which she had hoped for, her sister gave her a view of Jerusalem from the Mount of Olives, which is not quite the same thing. The revenge of an elder sister may be long in coming, but, like a South-Eastern express, it arrives in its own good time.

The friends of the Woman tried to dissuade her from over-indulgence in the practice, but she said she was wedded to the truth; whereupon it was remarked that it was scarcely logical to be so much together in public. (No really provident woman lunches regularly with her husband if she wishes to burst upon him as a revelation at dinner. He must have time to forget; an afternoon is not enough.) And after a while her friends began to thin out in patches. Her passion for the truth was not compatible with a large visiting-list. For instance, she told Miriam Klopstock *exactly* how she looked at the Ilexes' ball. Certainly Miriam had asked for her candid opinion, but the Woman prayed in church every Sunday for peace in our time, and it was not consistent.

It was unfortunate, everyone agreed, that she had no family; with a child or two in the house, there is an unconscious check upon too free an indulgence in the truth. Children are given us to discourage our better emotions. That is why the stage, with all its efforts, can never be as artificial as life; even in an Ibsen[78] drama one must reveal to the audience things that one would suppress before the children or servants.

Fate may have ordained the truth-telling from the commencement and should justly bear some of the blame; but in having no children the Woman was guilty, at least, of contributory negligence.

Little by little she felt she was becoming a slave to what had once been merely an idle propensity; and one day she knew. Every woman tells ninety per cent, of the truth to her dressmaker; the other ten per cent is the irreducible minimum of deception beyond which no self-respecting client trespasses. Madame Draga's establishment was a meeting-ground for naked truths and overdressed fictions, and it was here, the Woman felt, that she might make a final effort to recall the artless mendacity of past days. Madame herself was in an inspiring mood, with the air of a sphinx who knew all things and preferred to forget most of them. As a War Minister she might have been celebrated, but she was content to be merely rich.

"If I take it in here, and—Miss Howard, one moment, if you please—and there, and round like this—so—I really think you will find it quite easy."

The Woman hesitated; it seemed to require such a small effort to simply acquiesce in Madame's views. But habit had become too strong. "I'm afraid," she faltered, "it's just the least little bit in the world too—"

And by that least little bit she measured the deeps and eternities of her thraldom to fact. Madame was not best pleased at being contradicted on a professional matter, and when Madame lost her temper you usually found it afterwards in the bill.

And at last the dreadful thing came, as the Woman had foreseen all along that it must; it was one of those paltry little truths with which she harried her waking hours. On a raw Wednesday morning, in a few ill-chosen words, she told the cook that

---

[78] Norwegian dramatist (1828-1906); his plays scandalised on account of their refusal to be moral.

she drank. She remembered the scene afterwards as vividly as though it had been painted in her mind by Abbey.[79] The cook was a good cook, as cooks go; and as cooks go she went.

Miriam Klopstock came to lunch the next day. Women and elephants never forget an injury.

Reginald's Drama

Reginald closed his eyes with the elaborate weariness of one who has rather nice eyelashes and thinks it useless to conceal the fact.

"One of these days," he said, "I shall write a really great drama. No one will understand the drift of it, but everyone will go back to their homes with a vague feeling of dissatisfaction with their lives and surroundings. Then they will put up new wall-papers and forget."

"But how about those that have oak panelling all over the house?" said the Other.

"They can always put down new stair-carpets," pursued Reginald, "and, anyhow, I'm not responsible for the audience having a happy ending. The play would be quite sufficient strain on one's energies. I should get a bishop to say it was immoral and beautiful—no dramatist has thought of that before, and everyone would come to condemn the bishop, and they would stay on out of sheer nervousness. After all, it requires a great deal of moral courage to leave in a marked manner in the middle of the second act, when your carriage isn't ordered till twelve. And it would commence with wolves worrying something on a lonely waste—you wouldn't see them, of course; but you would hear them snarling and scrunching, and I should arrange to have a wolfy fragrance suggested across the footlights. It would look so well on the programmes, 'Wolves in the first act, by Jamrach.'[80] And old Lady Whortleberry, who never misses a

---

[79] Edwin Austin Abbey (1852-1911), American painter and illustrator.

[80] Johann Christian Carl Jamrach (1815-1891), known better as Charles Jamrach, was a well-known German-born and London-based importer, breeder and seller of wild animals.

first night, would scream. She's always been nervous since she lost her first husband. He died quite abruptly while watching a county cricket match; two and a half inches of rain had fallen for seven runs, and it was supposed that the excitement killed him. Anyhow, it gave her quite a shock; it was the first husband she'd lost, you know, and now she always screams if anything thrilling happens too soon after dinner. And after the audience had heard the Whortleberry scream the thing would be fairly launched."

"And the plot?"

"The plot," said Reginald, "would be one of those little everyday tragedies that one sees going on all round one. In my mind's eye there is the case of the Mudge-Jervises, which in an unpretentious way has quite an Enoch Arden[81] intensity underlying it. They'd only been married some eighteen months or so, and circumstances had prevented their seeing much of each other. With him there was always a foursome or something that had to be played and replayed in different parts of the country, and she went in for slumming[82] quite as seriously as if it was a sport. With her, I suppose, it was. She belonged to the Guild of the Poor Dear Souls, and they hold the record for having nearly reformed a washerwoman. No one has ever really reformed a washerwoman, and that is why the competition is so keen. You can rescue charwomen by fifties with a little tea and personal magnetism, but with washerwomen it's different; wages are too high. This particular laundress, who came from Bermondsey or some such place, was really rather a hopeful venture, and they thought at last that she might be safely put in the window as a specimen of successful work. So they had her paraded at a drawing-room 'At Home' at Agatha Camelford's; it was sheer bad luck that some liqueur chocolates had been turned loose by

---

[81] Referring to the eponymous narrative poem by Tennyson, in which the protagonist goes to sea to provide for his wife and children. He is shipwrecked and lives for ten years as a castaway. On returning home he finds his wife has remarried and one child has died. He dies of a broken heart without revealing to his wife that he had survived.

[82] In the slang sense of "associating with loose women".

mistake among the refreshments—really liqueur chocolates, with very little chocolate. And of course the old soul found them out, and cornered the entire stock. It was like finding a whelk-stall in a desert, as she afterwards partially expressed herself. When the liqueurs began to take effect, she started to give them imitations of farmyard animals as they know them in Bermondsey. She began with a dancing bear, and you know Agatha doesn't approve of dancing, except at Buckingham Palace under proper supervision. And then she got up on the piano and gave them an organ monkey; I gather she went in for realism rather than a Maeterlinckian[83] treatment of the subject. Finally, she fell into the piano and said she was a parrot in a cage, and for an impromptu performance I believe she was very word-perfect; no one had heard anything like it, except Baroness Boobelstein who has attended sittings of the Austrian Reichsrath.[84] Agatha is trying the Rest-cure at Buxton."[85]

"But the tragedy?"

"Oh, the Mudge-Jervises. Well, they were getting along quite happily, and their married life was one continuous exchange of picture-postcards; and then one day they were thrown together on some neutral ground where foursomes and washerwomen overlapped, and discovered that they were hopelessly divided on the Fiscal Question.[86] They have thought it best to separate, and she is to have the custody of the Persian kittens for nine months in the year—they go back to him for the winter, when she is abroad. There you have the material for a

---

[83] See footnote 51.

[84] Imperial parliament. Relations between the Empire's various ethnic groups were so strained that whenever German-speaking deputies got up to speak, the Czech representatives would try to drown them out by banging on the desks and even playing musical instruments. Debates often ended in brawls. The Emperor had been forced several times to suspend the parliament and rule by decree.

[85] Spa town in Derbyshire.

[86] A long-running debate over protectionism versus free trade flared up again in 1903 when Joseph Chamberlain, Secretary of State for the Colonies, resigned from the Cabinet after they rejected his proposed 'tariff reform', which would have given preferential tax treatment to trade with the Empire. See 'Reginald on Tariffs' on page 35.

tragedy drawn straight from life—and the piece could be called 'The Price They Paid for Empire.' And of course one would have to work in studies of the struggle of hereditary tendency against environment and all that sort of thing. The woman's father could have been an Envoy to some of the smaller German Courts; that's where she'd get her passion for visiting the poor, in spite of the most careful upbringing. *C'est le premier pa qui compte*,[87] as the cuckoo said when it swallowed its foster-parent. That, I think, is quite clever."

"And the wolves?"

"Oh, the wolves would be a sort of elusive undercurrent in the background that would never be satisfactorily explained. After all, life teems with things that have no earthly reason. And whenever the characters could think of nothing brilliant to say about marriage or the War Office, they could open a window and listen to the howling of the wolves. But that would be very seldom."

Reginald on Tariffs

I'm not going to discuss the Fiscal Question[88] (said Reginald); I wish to be original. At the same time, I think one suffers more than one realises from the system of free imports. I should like, for instance, a really prohibitive duty put upon the partner who declares on a weak red suit and hopes for the best. Even a free outlet for compressed verbiage doesn't balance matters. And I think there should be a sort of bounty-fed export (is that the right expression?) of the people who impress on you that you ought to take life seriously. There are only two classes that really can't help taking life seriously—schoolgirls of thirteen and Hohenzollerns;[89] they might be exempt. Albanians come under another heading; they take life whenever they get the opportunity. The one Albanian that I was ever on speaking terms with

---

[87] Sic. Correctly spelt, the idiom means "It's the first step that counts". Reginald is punning on "pas" (French for "step") and "pa" in the sense of father.

[88] See note 86.

[89] The ruling royal family of Germany.

was rather a decadent example. He was a Christian and a grocer, and I don't fancy he had ever killed anybody. I didn't like to question him on the subject—that showed my delicacy. Mrs. Nicorax says I have no delicacy; she hasn't forgiven me about the mice. You see, when I was staying down there, a mouse used to cake-walk about my room half the night, and none of their silly patent traps seemed to take its fancy as a bijou residence, so I determined to appeal to the better side of it—which with mice is the inside. So I called it Percy, and put little delicacies down near its hole every night, and that kept it quiet while I read Max Nordau's *Degeneration*[90] and other reproving literature, and went to sleep. And now she says there is a whole colony of mice in that room.

That isn't where the indelicacy comes in. She went out riding with me, which was entirely her own suggestion, and as we were coming home through some meadows she made a quite unnecessary attempt to see if her pony would jump a rather messy sort of brook that was there. It wouldn't. It went with her as far as the water's edge, and from that point Mrs. Nicorax went on alone. Of course I had to fish her out from the bank, and my riding-breeches are not cut with a view to salmon-fishing—it's rather an art even to ride in them. Her habit-skirt was one of those open questions that need not be adhered to in emergencies, and on this occasion it remained behind in some waterweeds. She wanted me to fish about for that too, but I felt I had done enough Pharaoh's daughter business[91] for an October afternoon, and I was beginning to want my tea. So I bundled her up on to her pony, and gave her a lead towards home as fast as I cared to go. What with the wet and the unusual responsibility, her abridged costume did not stand the pace particularly well, and she got quite querulous when I shouted back that I had no pins with me—and no string. Some women expect so much from a fellow. When we got into the drive she

---

[90] Max Nordau (1849-1923). His highly controversial book *Degeneration* (1892) attacked what he perceived as the immorality in *fin-de-siècle* art, as well as other manifestations of modern life, and argued for censorship to prevent humanity degenerating both morally and physically.

[91] See Exodus 2:5.

REGINALD ON TARIFFS 37

wanted to go up the back way to the stables, but the ponies *know* they always get sugar at the front door, and I never attempt to hold a pulling pony; as for Mrs. Nicorax, it took her all she knew to keep a firm hand on her seceding garments, which, as her maid remarked afterwards, were more *tout* than *ensemble*.[92] Of course nearly the whole house-party were out on the lawn watching the sunset—the only day this month that it's occurred to the sun to show itself, as Mrs. Nic. viciously observed—and I shall never forget the expression on her husband's face as we pulled up. "My darling, this is too much!" was his first spoken comment; taking into consideration the state of her toilet, it was the most brilliant thing I had ever heard him say, and I went into the library to be alone and scream. Mrs. Nicorax says I have no delicacy.

Talking about tariffs, the lift-boy, who reads extensively between the landings, says it won't do to tax raw commodities. What, exactly, is a raw commodity? Mrs. Van Challaby says men are raw commodities till you marry them; after they've struck Mrs. Van C., I can fancy they pretty soon become a finished article. Certainly she's had a good deal of experience to support her opinion. She lost one husband in a railway accident, and mislaid another in the Divorce Court, and the current one has just got himself squeezed in a Beef Trust. "What was he doing in a Beef Trust, anyway?" she asked tearfully, and I suggested that perhaps he had an unhappy home. I only said it for the sake of making conversation; which it did. Mrs. Van Challaby said things about me which in her calmer moments she would have hesitated to spell. It's a pity people can't discuss fiscal matters without getting wild. However, she wrote next day to ask if I could get her a Yorkshire terrier of the size and shade that's being worn now, and that's as near as a woman can be expected to get to owning herself in the wrong. And she will tie a salmon-pink bow to its collar, and call it "Reggie," and take it with her everywhere—like poor Miriam Klopstock, who *would* take her

---

[92] *tout ensemble*: the whole effect (French). The pun is on "ensemble", which also means "together".

Chow with her to the bathroom, and while she was bathing it was playing at she-bears with her garments. Miriam is always late for breakfast, and she wasn't really missed till the middle of lunch.

However, I'm not going any further into the Fiscal Question. Only I should like to be protected from the partner with a weak red tendency.[93]

Reginald's Christmas Revel

They say (said Reginald) that there's nothing sadder than victory except defeat. If you've ever stayed with dull people during what is alleged to be the festive season, you can probably revise that saying. I shall never forget putting in a Christmas at the Babwolds'. Mrs. Babwold is some relation of my father's—a sort of to-be-left-till-called-for cousin—and that was considered sufficient reason for my having to accept her invitation at about the sixth time of asking; though why the sins of the father should be visited by the children—you won't find any notepaper in that drawer; that's where I keep old menus and first-night programmes.

Mrs. Babwold wears a rather solemn personality, and has never been known to smile, even when saying disagreeable things to her friends or making out the Stores list.[94] She takes her pleasures sadly. A state elephant at a Durbar[95] gives one a very similar impression. Her husband gardens in all weathers. When a man goes out in the pouring rain to brush caterpillars off rose-trees, I generally imagine his life indoors leaves something to be desired; anyway, it must be very unsettling for the caterpillars.

Of course there were other people there. There was a Major Somebody who had shot things in Lapland, or somewhere

---

[93] In bridge.

[94] A printed catalogue of goods at discount prices.

[95] A public ceremonial reception, originally one held by an Indian noble, but then taken over to refer to those organised by a British governor or viceroy.

of that sort; I forget what they were, but it wasn't for want of reminding. We had them cold with every meal almost, and he was continually giving us details of what they measured from tip to tip, as though he thought we were going to make them warm under-things for the winter. I used to listen to him with a rapt attention that I thought rather suited me, and then one day I quite modestly gave the dimensions of an okapi I had shot in the Lincolnshire fens. The Major turned a beautiful Tyrian scarlet (I remember thinking at the time that I should like my bathroom hung in that colour), and I think that at that moment he almost found it in his heart to dislike me. Mrs. Babwold put on a first-aid-to-the-injured expression, and asked him why he didn't publish a book of his sporting reminiscences; it would be *so* interesting. She didn't remember till afterwards that he had given her two fat volumes on the subject, with his portrait and autograph as a frontispiece and an appendix on the habits of the Arctic mussel.

It was in the evening that we cast aside the cares and distractions of the day and really lived. Cards were thought to be too frivolous and empty a way of passing the time, so most of them played what they called a book game. You went out into the hall—to get an inspiration, I suppose—then you came in again with a muffler tied round your neck and looked silly, and the others were supposed to guess that you were *Wee MacGreegor*.[96] I held out against the inanity as long as I decently could, but at last, in a lapse of good-nature, I consented to masquerade as a book, only I warned them that it would take some time to carry out. They waited for the best part of forty minutes, while I went and played wineglass skittles with the page-boy in the pantry; you play it with a champagne cork, you know, and the one who knocks down the most glasses without breaking them wins. I won, with four unbroken out of seven; I think William suffered from over-anxiousness. They were rather mad in the drawing-room at my not having come back, and they weren't a bit paci-

---

[96] Scottish writer J.J. Bell (1871-1934) invented this character for his articles in the *Glasgow Evening Times*.

fied when I told them afterwards that I was *At the end of the passage*.[97]

"I never did like Kipling," was Mrs. Babwold's comment, when the situation dawned upon her. "I couldn't see anything clever in *Earthworms out of Tuscany*—or is that by Darwin?"[98]

Of course these games are very educational, but, personally, I prefer bridge.

On Christmas evening we were supposed to be specially festive in the Old English fashion. The hall was horribly draughty, but it seemed to be the proper place to revel in, and it was decorated with Japanese fans and Chinese lanterns, which gave it a very Old English effect. A young lady with a confidential voice favoured us with a long recitation about a little girl who died or did something equally hackneyed, and then the Major gave us a graphic account of a struggle he had with a wounded bear. I privately wished that the bears would win sometimes on these occasions; at least they wouldn't go vapouring about it afterwards. Before we had time to recover our spirits, we were indulged with some thought-reading by a young man whom one knew instinctively had a good mother and an indifferent tailor—the sort of young man who talks unflaggingly through the thickest soup, and smooths his hair dubiously as though he thought it might hit back. The thought-reading was rather a success; he announced that the hostess was thinking about poetry, and she admitted that her mind was dwelling on one of Austin's odes.[99] Which was near enough. I fancy she had been really wondering whether a scrag-end of mutton and some cold plum-pudding would do for the kitchen dinner next day. As a crowning dissipation, they all sat down to play progressive halma,[100] with milk-chocolate for prizes. I've been carefully brought up, and I don't like to play games of skill

---

[97] Short story by Rudyard Kipling.

[98] There is no work by Kipling with this title. However, Darwin's last book was about earthworms (published 1881).

[99] Minor poet (1835-1913) who was appointed Poet Laureate in 1896, an honour that many felt his work did not justify.

[100] A board game, invented in 1883, similar to Chinese checkers.

for milk-chocolate, so I invented a headache and retired from the scene. I had been preceded a few minutes earlier by Miss Langshan-Smith, a rather formidable lady, who always got up at some uncomfortable hour in the morning, and gave you the impression that she had been in communication with most of the European Governments before breakfast. There was a paper pinned on her door with a signed request that she might be called particularly early on the morrow. Such an opportunity does not come twice in a lifetime. I covered up everything except the signature with another notice, to the effect that before these words should meet the eye she would have ended a misspent life, was sorry for the trouble she was giving, and would like a military funeral. A few minutes later I violently exploded an air-filled paper bag on the landing, and gave a stage moan that could have been heard in the cellars. Then I pursued my original intention and went to bed. The noise those people made in forcing open the good lady's door was positively indecorous; she resisted gallantly, but I believe they searched her for bullets for about a quarter of an hour, as if she had been an historic battlefield.

I hate travelling on Boxing Day, but one must occasionally do things that one dislikes.

Reginald's Rubaiyat[101]

The other day (confided Reginald), when I was killing time in the bathroom and making bad resolutions for the New Year, it occurred to me that I would like to be a poet. The chief qualification, I understand, is that you must be born. Well, I hunted up my birth certificate, and found that I was all right on that score, and then I got to work on a Hymn to the New Year, which struck me as having possibilities. It suggested extremely unusual things to absolutely unlikely people, which I believe is the art of first-class catering in any department. Quite the best verse in it went something like this:

---
[101] See introduction.

> "Have you heard the groan of a gravelled grouse,
> Or the snarl of a snaffled snail
> (Husband or mother, like me, or spouse)
> Have you lain a-creep in the darkened house
> Where the wounded wombats wail?"

It was quite improbable that anyone had, you know, and that's where it stimulated the imagination and took people out of their narrow, humdrum selves. No one has ever called me narrow or humdrum, but even I felt worked up now and then at the thought of that house with the stricken wombats in it. It simply wasn't nice. But the editors were unanimous in leaving it alone; they said the thing had been done before and done worse, and that the market for that sort of work was extremely limited.

It was just on the top of that discouragement that the Duchess wanted me to write something in her album—something Persian, you know, and just a little bit decadent—and I thought a quatrain on an unwholesome egg would meet the requirements of the case. So I started in with—

> "Cackle, cackle, little hen,
> How I wonder if and when
> Once you laid the egg that I
> Met, alas! too late. Amen."[102]

The Duchess objected to the Amen, which I thought gave an air of forgiveness and *chose jugée* to the whole thing; also she said it wasn't Persian enough, as though I were trying to sell her a kitten whose mother had married for love rather than pedigree. So I recast it entirely, and the new version read—

> "The hen that laid thee moons ago, who knows
> In what Dead Yesterday[103] her shades repose;

---

[102] Apart from the first, all of Reginald's poems imitate the AABA rhyme scheme FitzGerald used in his Omar Khayyám translations.

[103] The phrase "Dead Yesterday" is taken directly from FitzGerald (ruba'i number 37 in the first edition).

REGINALD'S RUBAIYAT

> To some election turn thy waning span
> And rain thy rottenness on fiscal foes."

I thought there was enough suggestion of decay in that to satisfy a jackal, and to me there was something infinitely pathetic and appealing in the idea of the egg having a sort of St. Luke's summer[104] of commercial usefulness. But the Duchess begged me to leave out any political allusions; she's the president of a Women's Something or other, and she said it might be taken as an endorsement of deplorable methods. I never can remember which Party Irene discourages with her support, but I shan't forget an occasion when I was staying at her place and she gave me a pamphlet to leave at the house of a doubtful voter, and some grapes and things for a woman who was suffering from a chill on the top of a patent medicine. I thought it much cleverer to give the grapes to the former and the political literature to the sick woman, and the Duchess was quite absurdly annoyed about it afterwards. It seems the leaflet was addressed "To those about to wobble"—I wasn't responsible for the silly title of the thing—and the woman never recovered; anyway, the voter was completely won over by the grapes and jellies, and I think that should have balanced matters. The Duchess called it bribery, and said it might have compromised the candidate she was supporting; he was expected to subscribe to church funds and chapel funds, and football and cricket clubs and regattas, and bazaars and beanfeasts and bellringers, and poultry shows and ploughing matches, and reading-rooms and choir outings, and shooting trophies and testimonials, and anything of that sort; but bribery would not have been tolerated.

I fancy I have perhaps more talent for electioneering than for poetry, and I was really getting extended over this quatrain business. The egg began to be unmanageable, and the Duchess suggested something with a French literary ring about it. I hunted back in my mind for the most familiar French classic that I could

---

[104] Indian summer (St. Luke's day is 18th October).

take liberties with, and after a little exercise of memory I turned out the following:-

> "Hast thou the pen that once the gardener had?
> I have it not; and know, these pears are bad.
> Oh, larger than the horses of the Prince
> Are those the general drives in Kaikobad."

Even that didn't altogether satisfy Irene; I fancy the geography of it puzzled her. She probably thought Kaikobad was an unfashionable German spa,[105] where you'd meet matrimonial bargain-hunters and emergency Servian[106] kings. My temper was beginning to slip its moorings by that time. I look rather nice when I lose my temper. (I hoped you would say I lose it very often. I mustn't monopolise the conversation.)

"Of course, if you want something really Persian and passionate, with red wine and bulbuls in it," I went on to suggest; but she grabbed the book away from me.

"Not for worlds. Nothing with red wine or passion in it. Dear Agatha gave me the album, and she would be mortified to the quick—"

I said I didn't believe Agatha had a quick, and we got quite heated in arguing the matter. Finally, the Duchess declared I shouldn't write anything nasty in her book, and I said I wouldn't write anything in her nasty book, so there wasn't a very wide point of difference between us. For the rest of the afternoon I pretended to be sulking, but I was really working back to that quatrain, like a fox-terrier that's buried a deferred lunch in a private flower-bed. When I got an opportunity I hunted up Agatha's autograph, which had the front page all to itself, and, copying her prim handwriting as well as I could, I inserted above it the following Thibetan fragment:

---

[105] Has Reginald (or Munro?) slipped up? There is no place called Kaikobad. The word does occur in FitzGerald's *Rubáiyát* but there it refers to a king of ancient Persia.

[106] Alternative spelling of "Serbian". Serbian kings tended to have short and ill-fated reigns. In the last hundred years nearly all had abdicated or been deposed or assassinated. Reginald is mischievously suggesting one could never know when a new one might be needed.

"With Thee, oh, my Beloved, to do a dâk

(a dâk I believe is a sort of uncomfortable post-journey)[107]

On the pack-saddle of a grunting yak,
With never room for chilling chaperone,
'Twere better than a Panhard in the Park."[108]

That Agatha would get on to a yak in company with a lover even in the comparative seclusion of Thibet is unthinkable. I very much doubt if she'd do it with her own husband in the privacy of the Simplon tunnel.[109] But poetry, as I've remarked before, should always stimulate the imagination.

By the way, when you asked me the other day to dine with you on the 14th, I said I was dining with the Duchess. Well, I'm not. I'm dining with you.

The Innocence of Reginald

Reginald slid a carnation of the newest shade into the buttonhole of his latest lounge coat, and surveyed the result with approval. "I am just in the mood," he observed, "to have my portrait painted by someone with an unmistakable future. So comforting to go down to posterity as 'Youth with a Pink Carnation' in catalogue-company with 'Child with Bunch of Primroses,' and all that crowd."

"Youth," said the Other, "should suggest innocence."

"But never act on the suggestion. I don't believe the two ever really go together. People talk vaguely about the innocence of a little child, but they take mighty good care not to let it out of their sight for twenty minutes. The watched pot never boils over. I knew a boy once who really was innocent; his parents were in Society, but they never gave him a moment's anxiety from his

---

[107] Almost: it is the postal system in India, originally using a system of runners.

[108] Panhard was a French car-manufacturing company.

[109] Railway tunnel between Switzerland and Italy.

infancy. He believed in company prospectuses, and in the purity of elections, and in women marrying for love, and even in a system for winning at roulette. He never quite lost his faith in it, but he dropped more money than his employers could afford to lose. When last I heard of him, he was believing in his innocence; the jury weren't. All the same, I really am innocent just now of something everyone accuses me of having done, and so far as I can see, their accusations will remain unfounded."

"Rather an unexpected attitude for you."

"I love people who do unexpected things. Didn't you always adore the man who slew a lion in a pit on a snowy day?[110] But about this unfortunate innocence. Well, quite long ago, when I'd been quarrelling with more people than usual, you among the number—it must have been in November, I never quarrel with you too near Christmas—I had an idea that I'd like to write a book. It was to be a book of personal reminiscences, and was to leave out nothing."

"Reginald!"

"Exactly what the Duchess said when I mentioned it to her. I was provoking and said nothing, and the next thing, of course, was that everyone heard that I'd written the book and got it in the press. After that, I might have been a gold-fish in a glass bowl for all the privacy I got. People attacked me about it in the most unexpected places, and implored or commanded me to leave out things that I'd forgotten had ever happened. I sat behind Miriam Klopstock one night in the dress circle at His Majesty's,[111] and she began at once about the incident of the Chow dog in the bathroom, which she insisted must be struck out. We had to argue it in a disjointed fashion, because some of the people wanted to listen to the play, and Miriam takes nines in voices. They had to stop her playing in the 'Macaws' Hockey Club because you could hear what she thought when her shins got mixed up in a scrimmage for half a mile on a still day. They are called the Macaws because of their blue-and-yellow

---

[110] See 1 Chronicles 11:22.

[111] His Majesty's Theatre in London's West End, owned and managed by the impresario Herbert Beerbohm Tree.

costumes, but I understand there was nothing yellow about Miriam's language. I agreed to make one alteration, as I pretended I had got it a Spitz instead of a Chow, but beyond that I was firm. She megaphoned back two minutes later, 'You promised you would never mention it; don't you ever keep a promise?' When people had stopped glaring in our direction, I replied that I'd as soon think of keeping white mice. I saw her tearing little bits out of her programme for a minute or two, and then she leaned back and snorted, 'You're not the boy I took you for,' as though she were an eagle arriving at Olympus with the wrong Ganymede.[112] That was her last audible remark, but she went on tearing up her programme and scattering the pieces around her, till one of her neighbours asked with immense dignity whether she should send for a wastepaper basket. I didn't stay for the last act.

"Then there is Mrs.—oh, I never can remember her name; she lives in a street that the cabmen have never heard of, and is at home on Wednesdays.[113] She frightened me horribly once at a private view by saying mysteriously, 'I oughtn't to be here, you know; this is one of my days.' I thought she meant that she was subject to periodical outbreaks and was expecting an attack at any moment. So embarrassing if she had suddenly taken it into her head that she was Cesar Borgia or St. Elizabeth of Hungary. That sort of thing would make one unpleasantly conspicuous even at a private view. However, she merely meant to say that it was Wednesday, which at the moment was incontrovertible. Well, she's on quite a different tack to the Klopstock. She doesn't visit anywhere very extensively, and, of course, she's awfully keen for me to drag in an incident that occurred at one of the Beauwhistle garden-parties, when she says she accidentally hit the shins of a Serene Somebody or other with a croquet mallet and that he swore at her in German. As a matter

---

[112] In Greek mythology, Ganymede was a beautiful boy who was abducted by an eagle and brought to Olympus to serve as Zeus' cup-bearer.

[113] Lady Colin Campbell in *Etiquette of Good Society* (1893) explains that "Many ladies adopt the plan of always being at home on stated afternoons".

of fact, he went on discoursing on the Gordon-Bennett affair[114] in French. (I never can remember if it's a new submarine or a divorce. Of course, how stupid of me!) To be disagreeably exact, I fancy she missed him by about two inches—over-anxiousness, probably—but she likes to think she hit him. I've felt that way with a partridge which I always imagine keeps on flying strong, out of false pride, till it's the other side of the hedge. She said she could tell me everything she was wearing on the occasion. I said I didn't want my book to read like a laundry list, but she explained that she didn't mean those sort of things.

"And there's the Chilworth boy, who can be charming as long as he's content to be stupid and wear what he's told to; but he gets the idea now and then that he'd like to be epigrammatic, and the result is like watching a rook trying to build a nest in a gale. Since he got wind of the book, he's been persecuting me to work in something of his about the Russians and the Yalu Peril,[115] and is quite sulky because I won't do it.

"Altogether, I think it would be rather a brilliant inspiration if you were to suggest a fortnight in Paris."

---

[114] Gordon Bennett (1841-1918) was an American newspaper publisher and international playboy.

[115] Punning on "Yellow Peril". Yalu is a river between Korea and China and was the site of several military conflicts. Reginald's friend is referring to the events of the Russo-Japanese War of 1904-1905.

Reginald in Russia (1910)

Reginald In Russia

Reginald sat in a corner of the Princess's salon and tried to forgive the furniture, which started out with an obvious intention of being Louis Quinze, but relapsed at frequent intervals into Wilhelm II.[116]

He classified the Princess with that distinct type of woman that looks as if it habitually went out to feed hens in the rain.

Her name was Olga; she kept what she hoped and believed to be a fox-terrier, and professed what she thought were Socialist opinions. It is not necessary to be called Olga if you are a Russian Princess; in fact, Reginald knew quite a number who were called Vera; but the fox-terrier and the Socialism are essential.

"The Countess Lomshen keeps a bull-dog," said the Princess suddenly. "In England is it more chic to have a bull-dog than a fox-terrier?"

Reginald threw his mind back over the canine fashions of the last ten years and gave an evasive answer.

"Do you think her handsome, the Countess Lomshen?" asked the Princess.

Reginald thought the Countess's complexion suggested an exclusive diet of macaroons and pale sherry. He said so.

"But that cannot be possible," said the Princess triumphantly; "I've seen her eating fish-soup at Donon's."[117]

The Princess always defended a friend's complexion if it was really bad. With her, as with a great many of her sex, charity began at homeliness and did not generally progress much farther.

Reginald withdrew his macaroon and sherry theory, and became interested in a case of miniatures.

"That?" said the Princess; "that is the old Princess Lorikoff. She lived in Millionaya Street, near the Winter Palace, and was

---

[116] Furniture made during the reign of Louis the Fifteenth (Louis Quinze) of France (1723–1774) is considered an extremely fine style. "Wilhelm II style" would have meant modern furniture made during the current German Kaiser's reign (from 1888).

[117] One of St. Petersburg's best and most fashionable restaurants, founded 1849 at 24 Moika River Embankment.

one of the Court ladies of the old Russian school. Her knowledge of people and events was extremely limited; but she used to patronise every one who came in contact with her. There was a story that when she died and left the Millionaya for Heaven she addressed St. Peter in her formal staccato French: 'Je suis la Princesse Lor-i-koff. Il me donne grand plaisir à faire votre connaissance. Je vous en prie me presenter au Bon Dieu.'[118] St. Peter made the desired introduction, and the Princess addressed le Bon Dieu: 'Je suis la Princesse Lor-i-koff. Il me donne grand plaisir à faire votre connaissance. On a souvent parlé de vous a l'église de la rue Million.' "[119]

"Only the old and the clergy of Established churches know how to be flippant gracefully," commented Reginald; "which reminds me that in the Anglican Church in a certain foreign capital, which shall be nameless, I was present the other day when one of the junior chaplains was preaching in aid of distressed somethings or other, and he brought a really eloquent passage to a close with the remark, 'The tears of the afflicted, to what shall I liken them—to diamonds?' The other junior chaplain, who had been dozing out of professional jealousy, awoke with a start and asked hurriedly, 'Shall I play to diamonds, partner?' It didn't improve matters when the senior chaplain remarked dreamily but with painful distinctness, 'Double diamonds.' Every one looked at the preacher, half expecting him to redouble, but he contented himself with scoring what points he could under the circumstances."

"You English are always so frivolous," said the Princess. "In Russia we have too many troubles to permit of our being light-hearted."

Reginald gave a delicate shiver, such as an Italian greyhound might give in contemplating the approach of an ice age of which he personally disapproved, and resigned himself to the inevitable political discussion.

---

[118] "I am the Princess Lor-i-koff. I am very pleased to meet you. Please introduce me to the good Lord."

[119] "I am the Princess Lor-i-koff. I am very pleased to meet you. One often spoke of you at the church of Million Street."

"Nothing that you hear about us in England is true," was the Princess's hopeful beginning.

"I always refused to learn Russian geography at school," observed Reginald; "I was certain some of the names must be wrong."

"Everything is wrong with our system of government," continued the Princess placidly. "The Bureaucrats think only of their pockets, and the people are exploited and plundered in every direction, and everything is mismanaged."

"With us," said Reginald, "a Cabinet usually gets the credit of being depraved and worthless beyond the bounds of human conception by the time it has been in office about four years."

"But if it is a bad Government you can turn it out at the elections," argued the Princess.

"As far as I remember, we generally do," said Reginald.

"But here it is dreadful, every one goes to such extremes. In England you never go to extremes."

"We go to the Albert Hall," explained Reginald.

"There is always a see-saw with us between repression and violence," continued the Princess; "and the pity of it is the people are really not in the least inclined to be anything but peaceable. Nowhere will you find people more good-natured, or family circles where there is more affection."

"There I agree with you," said Reginald. "I know a boy who lives somewhere on the French Quay[120] who is a case in point. His hair curls naturally, especially on Sundays, and he plays bridge well, even for a Russian, which is saying much. I don't think he has any other accomplishments, but his family affection is really of a very high order. When his maternal grandmother died he didn't go as far as to give up bridge altogether, but he declared on nothing but black suits for the next three months. That, I think, was really beautiful."

The Princess was not impressed.

"I think you must be very self-indulgent and live only for amusement," she said, "a life of pleasure-seeking and

---

[120] Near the Summer Garden in St. Petersburg.

card-playing and dissipation brings only dissatisfaction. You will find that out some day."

"Oh, I know it turns out that way sometimes," assented Reginald. "Forbidden fizz is often the sweetest."

But the remark was wasted on the Princess, who preferred champagne that had at least a suggestion of dissolved barley-sugar.

"I hope you will come and see me again," she said, in a tone that prevented the hope from becoming too infectious; adding as a happy afterthought, "you must come to stay with us in the country." Her particular part of the country was a few hundred versts[121] the other side of Tamboff,[122] with some fifteen miles of agrarian disturbance between her and the nearest neighbour. Reginald felt that there is some privacy which should be sacred from intrusion.

The Reticence Of Lady Anne

Egbert came into the large, dimly lit drawing-room with the air of a man who is not certain whether he is entering a dovecote or a bomb factory, and is prepared for either eventuality. The little domestic quarrel over the luncheon-table had not been fought to a definite finish, and the question was how far Lady Anne was in a mood to renew or forgo hostilities. Her pose in the arm-chair by the tea-table was rather elaborately rigid; in the gloom of a December afternoon Egbert's pince-nez did not materially help him to discern the expression of her face.

By way of breaking whatever ice might be floating on the surface he made a remark about a dim religious light. He or Lady Anne were accustomed to make that remark between 4.30 and 6 on winter and late autumn evenings; it was a part of their married life. There was no recognised rejoinder to it, and Lady Anne made none.

---

[121] Old Russian measurement of length; one verst was just over a kilometre.
[122] Or Tambov, 480 kilometres south-southeast of Moscow.

THE RETICENCE OF LADY ANNE

Don Tarquinio lay astretch on the Persian rug, basking in the firelight with superb indifference to the possible ill-humour of Lady Anne. His pedigree was as flawlessly Persian as the rug, and his ruff was coming into the glory of its second winter. The page-boy, who had Renaissance tendencies, had christened him Don Tarquinio.[123] Left to themselves, Egbert and Lady Anne would unfailingly have called him Fluff, but they were not obstinate.

Egbert poured himself out some tea. As the silence gave no sign of breaking on Lady Anne's initiative, he braced himself for another Yermak[124] effort.

"My remark at lunch had a purely academic application," he announced; "you seem to put an unnecessarily personal significance into it."

Lady Anne maintained her defensive barrier of silence. The bullfinch lazily filled in the interval with an air from *Iphigénie en Tauride*.[125] Egbert recognised it immediately, because it was the only air the bullfinch whistled, and he had come to them with the reputation for whistling it. Both Egbert and Lady Anne would have preferred something from *The Yeomen of the Guard*,[126] which was their favourite opera. In matters artistic they had a similarity of taste. They leaned towards the honest and explicit in art, a picture, for instance, that told its own story, with generous assistance from its title. A riderless warhorse with harness in obvious disarray, staggering into a courtyard full of pale swooning women, and marginally noted "Bad News", suggested to their minds a distinct interpretation of some military catastrophe. They could see what it was meant to convey, and explain it to friends of duller intelligence.

The silence continued. As a rule Lady Anne's displeasure became articulate and markedly voluble after four minutes

---

[123] 1905 novel by Frederick Rolfe (Baron Corvo) about a Renaissance man of fashion.

[124] An heroic effort. (Yermak Timofeyevich is a Russian national hero. He was a Cossack who led the Russian conquest of Siberia.)

[125] There are several operas with this name, the best known being Christoph Willibald Gluck's of 1779.

[126] A Savoy opera by Gilbert and Sullivan, first performed in 1888.

of introductory muteness. Egbert seized the milk-jug and poured some of its contents into Don Tarquinio's saucer; as the saucer was already full to the brim an unsightly overflow was the result. Don Tarquinio looked on with a surprised interest that evanesced into elaborate unconsciousness when he was appealed to by Egbert to come and drink up some of the spilt matter. Don Tarquinio was prepared to play many roles in life, but a vacuum carpet-cleaner was not one of them.

"Don't you think we're being rather foolish?" said Egbert cheerfully.

If Lady Anne thought so she didn't say so.

"I dare say the fault has been partly on my side," continued Egbert, with evaporating cheerfulness. "After all, I'm only human, you know. You seem to forget that I'm only human."

He insisted on the point, as if there had been unfounded suggestions that he was built on Satyr[127] lines, with goat continuations where the human left off.

The bullfinch recommenced its air from *Iphigénie en Tauride*. Egbert began to feel depressed. Lady Anne was not drinking her tea. Perhaps she was feeling unwell. But when Lady Anne felt unwell she was not wont to be reticent on the subject. "No one knows what I suffer from indigestion" was one of her favourite statements; but the lack of knowledge can only have been caused by defective listening; the amount of information available on the subject would have supplied material for a monograph.

Evidently Lady Anne was not feeling unwell.

Egbert began to think he was being unreasonably dealt with; naturally he began to make concessions.

"I dare say," he observed, taking as central a position on the hearth-rug as Don Tarquinio could be persuaded to concede him, "I may have been to blame. I am willing, if I can thereby restore things to a happier standpoint, to undertake to lead a better life."

---

[127] Or faun, a creature in Roman mythology, human to the waist with the hindquarters and legs of a goat beneath.

He wondered vaguely how it would be possible. Temptations came to him, in middle age, tentatively and without insistence, like a neglected butcher-boy who asks for a Christmas box[128] in February for no more hopeful reason that than he didn't get one in December. He had no more idea of succumbing to them than he had of purchasing the fish-knives and fur boas that ladies are impelled to sacrifice through the medium of advertisement columns during twelve months of the year. Still, there was something impressive in this unasked-for renunciation of possibly latent enormities.

Lady Anne showed no sign of being impressed.

Egbert looked at her nervously through his glasses. To get the worst of an argument with her was no new experience. To get the worst of a monologue was a humiliating novelty.

"I shall go and dress for dinner," he announced in a voice into which he intended some shade of sternness to creep.

At the door a final access of weakness impelled him to make a further appeal.

"Aren't we being very silly?"

"A fool," was Don Tarquinio's mental comment as the door closed on Egbert's retreat. Then he lifted his velvet forepaws in the air and leapt lightly on to a bookshelf immediately under the bullfinch's cage. It was the first time he had seemed to notice the bird's existence, but he was carrying out a long-formed theory of action with the precision of mature deliberation. The bullfinch, who had fancied himself something of a despot, depressed himself of a sudden into a third of his normal displacement; then he fell to a helpless wing-beating and shrill cheeping. He had cost twenty-seven shillings without the cage, but Lady Anne made no sign of interfering. She had been dead for two hours.

---

[128] Servants and tradespeople were traditionally given a gift on the 26th December or the first weekday after Christmas Day.

The Lost Sanjak[129]

The prison Chaplain entered the condemned's cell for the last time, to give such consolation as he might.

"The only consolation I crave for," said the condemned, "is to tell my story in its entirety to some one who will at least give it a respectful hearing."

"We must not be too long over it," said the Chaplain, looking at his watch.

The condemned repressed a shiver and commenced.

"Most people will be of opinion that I am paying the penalty of my own violent deeds. In reality I am a victim to a lack of specialisation in my education and character."

"Lack of specialisation!" said the Chaplain.

"Yes. If I had been known as one of the few men in England familiar with the fauna of the Outer Hebrides, or able to repeat stanzas of Camoëns'[130] poetry in the original, I should have had no difficulty in proving my identity in the crisis when my identity became a matter of life and death for me. But my education was merely a moderately good one, and my temperament was of the general order that avoids specialisation. I know a little in a general way about gardening and history and old masters, but I could never tell you off-hand whether 'Stella van der Loopen' was a chrysanthemum or a heroine of the American War of Independence, or something by Romney in the Louvre."[131]

The Chaplain shifted uneasily in his seat. Now that the alternatives had been suggested they all seemed dreadfully possible.

"I fell in love, or thought I did, with the local doctor's wife," continued the condemned. "Why I should have done so, I cannot say, for I do not remember that she possessed any particular attractions of mind or body. On looking back at past events if seems to me that she must have been distinctly ordinary, but I

---

[129] A 'sanjak' was a type of administrative district in the Ottoman Empire. In this case—as becomes clear later— the Sanjak of Novi-Bazar (or Novi-Pazar) in what is now Serbia and Montenegro is meant.

[130] Portuguese poet (1524-1580).

[131] It is none of these.

suppose the doctor had fallen in love with her once, and what man had done man can do. She appeared to be pleased with the attentions which I paid her, and to that extent I suppose I might say she encouraged me, but I think she was honestly unaware that I meant anything more than a little neighbourly interest. When one is face to face with Death one wishes to be just."

The Chaplain murmured approval. "At any rate, she was genuinely horrified when I took advantage of the doctor's absence one evening to declare what I believed to be my passion. She begged me to pass out of her life, and I could scarcely do otherwise than agree, though I hadn't the dimmest idea of how it was to be done. In novels and plays I knew it was a regular occurrence, and if you mistook a lady's sentiments or intentions you went off to India and did things on the frontier as a matter of course. As I stumbled along the doctor's carriage-drive I had no very clear idea as to what my line of action was to be, but I had a vague feeling that I must look at the *Times* Atlas before going to bed. Then, on the dark and lonely highway, I came suddenly on a dead body."

The Chaplain's interest in the story visibly quickened.

"Judging by the clothes it wore, the corpse was that of a Salvation Army captain. Some shocking accident seemed to have struck him down, and the head was crushed and battered out of all human semblance. Probably, I thought, a motor-car fatality; and then, with a sudden overmastering insistence, came another thought, that here was a remarkable opportunity for losing my identity and passing out of the life of the doctor's wife for ever. No tiresome and risky voyage to distant lands, but a mere exchange of clothes and identity with the unknown victim of an unwitnessed accident. With considerable difficulty I undressed the corpse, and clothed it anew in my own garments. Any one who has valeted a dead Salvation Army captain in an uncertain light will appreciate the difficulty. With the idea, presumably, of inducing the doctor's wife to leave her husband's roof-tree for some habitation which would be run at my expense, I had crammed my pockets with a store of banknotes, which represented a good deal of my immediate worldly wealth. When, therefore, I stole away into the world in the guise of a nameless Salvationist, I was not without resources which would easily support so humble a role for a considerable period. I tramped to a neighbouring market-town, and, late as the hour was, the production of a few shillings procured me supper and a night's lodging in a cheap coffee-house. The next day I started forth on an aimless course of wandering from one small town to another. I was already somewhat disgusted with the upshot of my sudden freak; in a few hours' time I was considerably more so. In the contents-bill of a local news sheet I read the announcement of my own murder at the hands of some person unknown; on buying a copy of the paper for a detailed account of the tragedy, which at first had aroused in me a certain grim amusement, I found that the deed ascribed to a wandering Salvationist of doubtful antecedents, who had been seen lurking in the roadway near the scene of the crime. I was no longer amused. The matter promised to be embarrassing. What I had mistaken for a motor accident was evidently a case of savage assault and murder, and, until the real culprit was found, I should have much difficulty in explaining my intrusion into the affair. Of course I could establish my own identity; but how, without disagreeably involving the doctor's wife, could I give any adequate reason for changing clothes with the murdered man? While my brain worked feverishly at this problem, I subconsciously obeyed a secondary instinct–to get as far away as possible from the scene of the crime, and to get rid at all costs of my incriminating uniform. There I found a difficulty. I tried two or three obscure clothes shops, but my entrance invariably aroused an attitude of hostile suspicion in the proprietors, and on one excuse or another they avoided serving me with the now ardently desired change of clothing. The uniform that I had so thoughtlessly donned seemed as difficult to get out of as the fatal shirt of—[132] You know, I forget the creature's name."

---

[132] The shirt of Nessus, in Greek mythology, was a garment dipped in the poisonous blood of the centaur Nessus, which killed Heracles when he put it on.

"Yes, yes," said the Chaplain hurriedly. "Go on with your story."

"Somehow, until I could get out of those compromising garments, I felt it would not be safe to surrender myself to the police. The thing that puzzled me was why no attempt was made to arrest me, since there was no question as to the suspicion which followed me, like an inseparable shadow, wherever I went. Stares, nudgings, whisperings, and even loud-spoken remarks of 'that's 'im' greeted my every appearance, and the meanest and most deserted eating-house that I patronised soon became filled with a crowd of furtively watching customers. I began to sympathise with the feeling of Royal personages trying to do a little private shopping under the unsparing scrutiny of an irrepressible public. And still, with all this inarticulate shadowing, which weighed on my nerves almost worse than open hostility would have done, no attempt was made to interfere with my liberty. Later on I discovered the reason. At the time of the murder on the lonely highway a series of important bloodhound trials had been taking place in the near neighbourhood, and some dozen and a half couples of trained animals had been put on the track of the supposed murderer–on my track. One of our most public-spirited London dailies had offered a princely prize to the owner of the pair that should first track me down, and betting on the chances of the respective competitors became rife throughout the land. The dogs ranged far and wide over about thirteen counties, and though my own movements had become by this time perfectly well-known to police and public alike, the sporting instincts of the nation stepped in to prevent my premature arrest. "Give the dogs a chance," was the prevailing sentiment, whenever some ambitious local constable wished to put an end to my drawn-out evasion of justice. My final capture by the winning pair was not a very dramatic episode, in fact, I'm not sure that they would have taken any notice of me if I hadn't spoken to them and patted them, but the event gave rise to an extraordinary amount of partisan excitement. The owner of the pair who were next nearest up at the finish was an American, and he lodged a protest on the ground that an otterhound had married into the family of the winning pair six generations ago, and that the prize had been offered to the first pair of bloodhounds to capture the murderer, and that a dog that had 1/64th part of otterhound blood in it couldn't technically be considered a bloodhound. I forget how the matter was ultimately settled, but it aroused a tremendous amount of acrimonious discussion on both sides of the Atlantic. My own contribution to the controversy consisted in pointing out that the whole dispute was beside the mark, as the actual murderer had not yet been captured; but I soon discovered that on this point there was not the least divergence of public or expert opinion. I had looked forward apprehensively to the proving of my identity and the establishment of my motives as a disagreeable necessity; I speedily found out that the most disagreeable part of the business was that it couldn't be done. When I saw in the glass the haggard and hunted expression which the experiences of the past few weeks had stamped on my erstwhile placid countenance, I could scarcely feel surprised that the few friends and relations I possessed refused to recognise me in my altered guise, and persisted in their obstinate but widely shared belief that it was I who had been done to death on the highway. To make matters worse, infinitely worse, an aunt of the really murdered man, an appalling female of an obviously low order of intelligence, identified me as her nephew, and gave the authorities a lurid account of my depraved youth and of her laudable but unavailing efforts to spank me into a better way. I believe it was even proposed to search me for fingerprints."

"But," said the Chaplain, "surely your educational attainments—"

"That was just the crucial point," said the condemned; "that was where my lack of specialisation told so fatally against me. The dead Salvationist, whose identity I had so lightly and so disastrously adopted, had possessed a veneer of cheap modern education. It should have been easy to demonstrate that my learning was on altogether another plane to his, but in my nervousness I bungled miserably over test after test that was put to me. The little French I had ever known deserted me; I could not render

THE LOST SANJAK 63

a simple phrase about the gooseberry of the gardener into that language, because I had forgotten the French for gooseberry."

The Chaplain again wriggled uneasily in his seat. "And then," resumed the condemned, "came the final discomfiture. In our village we had a modest little debating club, and I remembered having promised, chiefly, I suppose, to please and impress the doctor's wife, to give a sketchy kind of lecture on the Balkan Crisis. I had relied on being able to get up my facts from one or two standard works, and the back-numbers of certain periodicals. The prosecution had made a careful note of the circumstance that the man whom I claimed to be–and actually was–had posed locally as some sort of second-hand authority on Balkan affairs, and, in the midst of a string of questions on indifferent topics, the examining counsel asked me with a diabolical suddenness if I could tell the Court the whereabouts of Novibazar. I felt the question to be a crucial one; something told me that the answer was St. Petersburg or Baker Street.[133] I hesitated, looked helplessly round at the sea of tensely expectant faces, pulled myself together, and chose Baker Street. And then I knew that everything was lost. The prosecution had no difficulty in demonstrating that an individual, even moderately versed in the affairs of the Near East, could never have so unceremoniously dislocated Novibazar from its accustomed corner of the map. It was an answer which the Salvation Army captain might conceivably have made–and I made it. The circumstantial evidence connecting the Salvationist with the crime was overwhelmingly convincing, and I had inextricably identified myself with the Salvationist. And thus it comes to pass that in ten minutes' time I shall be hanged by the neck until I am dead in expiation of the murder of myself, which murder never took place, and of which, in any case, I am innocent."

When the Chaplain returned to his quarters some fifteen minutes later, the black flag was floating over the prison tower. Breakfast was waiting for him in the dining-room, but he

---

[133] Madame Tussaud's famous waxworks museum was originally located in the Baker Street Bazaar in London.

first passed into his library, and, taking up the *Times* Atlas, consulted a map of the Balkan Peninsula. "A thing like that," he observed, closing the volume with a snap, "might happen to any one."

The Sex That Doesn't Shop

The opening of a large new centre for West End shopping, particularly feminine shopping, suggests the reflection, Do women ever really shop? Of course, it is a well-attested fact that they go forth shopping as assiduously as a bee goes flower-visiting, but do they shop in the practical sense of the word? Granted the money, time, and energy, a resolute course of shopping transactions would naturally result in having one's ordinary domestic needs unfailingly supplied, whereas it is notorious that women servants (and housewives of all classes) make it almost a point of honour not to be supplied with everyday necessities. "We shall be out of starch by Thursday," they say with fatalistic foreboding, and by Thursday they are out of starch. They have predicted almost to a minute the moment when their supply would give out and if Thursday happens to be early closing day their triumph is complete. A shop where starch is stored for retail purposes possibly stands at their very door, but the feminine mind has rejected such an obvious source for replenishing a dwindling stock. "We don't deal there" places it at once beyond the pale of human resort. And it is noteworthy that, just as a sheep-worrying dog seldom molests the flocks in his near neighbourhood, so a woman rarely deals with shops in her immediate vicinity. The more remote the source of supply the more fixed seems to be the resolve to run short of the commodity. The Ark had probably not quitted its last moorings five minutes before some feminine voice gloatingly recorded a shortage of bird-seed. A few days ago two lady acquaintances of mine were confessing to some mental uneasiness because a friend had called just before lunch-time, and they had been unable to ask her to stop and share their meal, as (with a touch of legitimate pride) "there was nothing in the house." I pointed out that they lived in a street that bristled with provision shops and that it would have been easy to mobilise a very passable luncheon in less than five minutes. "That," they said with quiet dignity, "would not have occurred to us," and I felt that I had suggested something bordering on the indecent.

But it is in catering for her literary wants that a woman's shopping capacity breaks down most completely. If you have perchance produced a book which has met with some little measure of success, you are certain to get a letter from some lady whom you scarcely known to bow to, asking you "how it can be got." She knows the name of the book, its author, and who published it, but how to get into actual contact with it is still an unsolved problem to her. You write back pointing out that to have recourse to an ironmonger or a corn-dealer will only entail delay and disappointment, and suggest an application to a bookseller as the most hopeful thing you can think of. In a day or two she writes again: "It is all right; I have borrowed it from your aunt." Here, of course, we have an example of the Beyond-Shopper, one who has learned the Better Way, but the helplessness exists even when such bypaths of relief are closed. A lady who lives in the West End was expressing to me the other day her interest in West Highland terriers, and her desire to know more about the breed, so when, a few days later, I came across an exhaustive article on that subject in the current number of one of our best known outdoor-life weeklies, I mentioned that circumstance in a letter, giving the date of that number. "I cannot get the paper," was her telephoned response. And she couldn't. She lived in a city where newsagents are numbered, I suppose, by the thousand, and she must have passed dozens of such shops in her daily shopping excursions, but as far as she was concerned that article on West Highland terriers might as well have been written in a missal stored away in some Buddhist monastery in Eastern Thibet.[134]

The brutal directness of the masculine shopper arouses a certain combative derision in the feminine onlooker. A cat that

---

[134] A old way of spelling "Tibet".

spreads one shrew-mouse over the greater part of a long summer afternoon, and then possibly loses him, doubtless feels the same contempt for the terrier who compresses his rat into ten seconds of the strenuous life. I was finishing off a short list of purchases a few afternoons ago when I was discovered by a lady of my acquaintance whom, swerving aside from the lead given us by her godparents thirty years ago, we will call Agatha.

"You're surely not buying blotting-paper *here*?" she exclaimed in an agitated whisper, and she seemed so genuinely concerned that I stayed my hand.

"Let me take you to Winks and Pinks," she said as soon as we were out of the building: "they've got such lovely shades of blotting-paper—pearl and heliotrope and *momie*[135] and crushed—"

"But I want ordinary white blotting-paper," I said.

"Never mind. They know me at Winks and Pinks," she replied inconsequently. Agatha apparently has an idea that blotting-paper is only sold in small quantities to persons of known reputation, who may be trusted not to put it to dangerous or improper uses. After walking some two hundred yards she began to feel that her tea was of more immediate importance than my blotting-paper.

"What do you want blotting-paper for?" she asked suddenly. I explained patiently.

"I use it to dry up the ink of wet manuscript without smudging the writing. Probably a Chinese invention of the second century before Christ, but I'm not sure. The only other use for it that I can think of is to roll it into a ball for a kitten to play with."

"But you haven't got a kitten," said Agatha, with a feminine desire for stating the entire truth on most occasions.

"A stray one might come in at any moment," I replied.

Anyway, I didn't get the blotting-paper.

---

[135] A popular shade of brown.

The Blood-Feud Of Toad-Water

A WEST-COUNTRY EPIC[136]

The Cricks lived at Toad-Water; and in the same lonely upland spot Fate had pitched the home of the Saunderses, and for miles around these two dwellings there was never a neighbour or a chimney or even a burying-ground to bring a sense of cheerful communion or social intercourse. Nothing but fields and spinneys and barns, lanes and waste-lands. Such was Toad-Water; and, even so, Toad-Water had its history.

Thrust away in the benighted hinterland of a scattered market district, it might have been supposed that these two detached items of the Great Human Family would have leaned towards one another in a fellowship begotten of kindred circumstances and a common isolation from the outer world. And perhaps it had been so once, but the way of things had brought it otherwise. Indeed, otherwise. Fate, which had linked the two families in such unavoidable association of habitat, had ordained that the Crick household should nourish and maintain among its earthly possessions sundry head of domestic fowls, while to the Saunderses was given a disposition towards the cultivation of garden crops. Herein lay the material, ready to hand, for the coming of feud and ill-blood. For the grudge between the man of herbs and the man of live stock is no new thing; you will find traces of it in the fourth chapter of Genesis. And one sunny afternoon in late spring-time the feud came—came, as such things mostly do come, with seeming aimlessness and triviality. One of the Crick hens, in obedience to the nomadic instincts of her kind, wearied of her legitimate scatching-ground, and flew over the low wall that divided the holdings of the neighbours. And there, on the yonder side, with a hurried consciousness that her time and opportunities might be limited, the misguided bird scratched and scraped

---

[136] According to Saki's biographer A. J. Langguth, the basic facts of this story were true and were told to the Munro family by the local rector during their childhood in Devon (p. 69).

and beaked and delved in the soft yielding bed that had been prepared for the solace and well-being of a colony of seedling onions. Little showers of earth-mould and root-fibres went spraying before the hen and behind her, and every minute the area of her operations widened. The onions suffered considerably. Mrs. Saunders, sauntering at this luckless moment down the garden path, in order to fill her soul with reproaches at the iniquity of the weeds, which grew faster than she or her good man cared to remove them, stopped in mute discomfiture before the presence of a more magnificent grievance. And then, in the hour of her calamity, she turned instinctively to the Great Mother, and gathered in her capacious hands large clods of the hard brown soil that lay at her feet. With a terrible sincerity of purpose, though with a contemptible inadequacy of aim, she rained her earth bolts at the marauder, and the bursting pellets called forth a flood of cackling protest and panic from the hastily departing fowl. Calmness under misfortune is not an attribute of either hen-folk or womenkind, and while Mrs. Saunders declaimed over her onion bed such portions of the slang dictionary as are permitted by the Nonconformist conscience to be said or sung, the Vasco da Gama fowl was waking the echoes of Toad-Water with crescendo bursts of throat music which compelled attention to her griefs. Mrs. Crick had a long family, and was therefore licensed, in the eyes of her world, to have a short temper, and when some of her ubiquitous offspring had informed her, with the authority of eye-witnesses, that her neighbour had so far forgotten herself as to heave stones at her hen—her best hen, the best layer in the countryside—her thoughts clothed themselves in language "unbecoming to a Christian woman"—so at least said Mrs. Saunders, to whom most of the language was applied. Nor was she, on her part, surprised at Mrs. Crick's conduct in letting her hens stray into other body's gardens, and then abusing of them, seeing as how she remembered things against Mrs. Crick—and the latter simultaneously had recollections of lurking episodes in the past of Susan Saunders that were nothing to her credit. "Fond memory, when all things fade we fly to thee," and in the paling light of an April afternoon the two women confronted each other from their respective sides of the party wall, recalling with shuddering breath the blots and blemishes of their neighbour's family record. There was that aunt of Mrs. Crick's who had died a pauper in Exeter workhouse—every one knew that Mrs. Saunders' uncle on her mother's side drank himself to death—then there was that Bristol cousin of Mrs. Crick's! From the shrill triumph with which his name was dragged in, his crime must have been pilfering from a cathedral at least, but as both remembrancers were speaking at once it was difficult to distinguish his infamy from the scandal which beclouded the memory of Mrs. Saunders' brother's wife's mother—who may have been a regicide, and was certainly not a nice person as Mrs. Crick painted her. And then, with an air of accumulating and irresistible conviction, each belligerent informed the other that she was no lady—after which they withdrew in a great silence, feeling that nothing further remained to be said. The chaffinches clinked in the apple trees and the bees droned round the berberis bushes, and the waning sunlight slanted pleasantly across the garden plots, but between the neighbour households had sprung up a barrier of hate, permeating and permanent.

The male heads of the families were necessarily drawn into the quarrel, and the children on either side were forbidden to have anything to do with the unhallowed offspring of the other party. As they had to travel a good three miles along the same road to school every day, this was awkward, but such things have to be. Thus all communication between the households was sundered. Except the cats. Much as Mrs. Saunders might deplore it, rumour persistently pointed to the Crick he-cat as the presumable father of sundry kittens of which the Saunders she-cat was indisputably the mother. Mrs. Saunders drowned the kittens, but the disgrace remained.

Summer succeeded spring, and winter summer, but the feud outlasted the waning seasons. Once, indeed, it seemed as though the healing influences of religion might restore to Toad-Water its erstwhile peace; the hostile families found themselves side by side in the soul-kindling atmosphere of a Revival Tea, where hymns were blended with a beverage that came of tea-leaves and hot water and took after the latter parent, and where ghostly counsel was tempered by garnishings of solidly fashioned buns—and here, wrought up by the environment of festive piety, Mrs. Saunders so far unbent as to remark guardedly to Mrs. Crick that the evening had been a fine one. Mrs. Crick, under the influence of her ninth cup of tea and her fourth hymn, ventured on the hope that it might continue fine, but a maladroit allusion on the part of the Saunders good man to the backwardness of garden crops brought the Feud stalking forth from its corner with all its old bitterness. Mrs. Saunders joined heartily in the singing of the final hymn, which told of peace and joy and archangels and golden glories; but her thoughts were dwelling on the pauper aunt of Exeter.

Years have rolled away, and some of the actors in this wayside drama have passed into the Unknown; other onions have arisen, have flourished, have gone their way, and the offending hen has long since expiated her misdeeds and lain with trussed feet and a look of ineffable peace under the arched roof of Barnstaple market.

But the Blood-feud of Toad-Water survives to this day.

A Young Turkish Catastrophe[137]

[IN TWO SCENES]

The Minister for Fine Arts (to whose Department had been lately added the new sub-section of Electoral Engineering) paid a business visit to the Grand Vizier. According to Eastern etiquette they discoursed for a while on indifferent subjects. The minister only checked himself in time from making a passing reference to the Marathon Race, remembering that

---

[137] The Young Turkish Revolution of 1908 had rebelled against the absolutist system in the Ottoman Empire and forced the Sultan to agree to a constitutional parliamentary democracy.

the Vizier had a Persian grandmother and might consider any allusion to Marathon as somewhat tactless. Presently the Minister broached the subject of his interview.

"Under the new Constitution are women to have votes?" he asked suddenly.

"To have votes? Women?" exclaimed the Vizier in some astonishment. "My dear Pasha, the New Departure has a flavour of the absurd as it is; don't let's try and make it altogether ridiculous. Women have no souls and no intelligence; why on earth should they have votes?"

"I know it sounds absurd," said the Minister, "but they are seriously considering the idea in the West."

"Then they must have a larger equipment of seriousness than I gave them credit for. After a lifetime of specialised effort in maintaining my gravity I can scarcely restrain an inclination to smile at the suggestion. Why, out womenfolk in most cases don't know how to read or write. How could they perform the operation of voting?"

"They could be shown the names of the candidates and where to make their cross."

"I beg your pardon?" interrupted the Vizier.

"Their crescent, I mean," corrected the Minister. "It would be to the liking of the Young Turkish Party," he added.

"Oh, well," said the Vizier, "if we are to do the thing at all we may as well go the whole h—" he pulled up just as he was uttering the name of an unclean animal, and continued, "the complete camel. I will issue instructions that womenfolk are to have votes."

* * *

The poll was drawing to a close in the Lakoumistan division. The candidate of the Young Turkish Party was known to be three or four hundred votes ahead, and he was already drafting his address, returning thanks to the electors. His victory had been almost a foregone conclusion, for he had set in motion all the approved electioneering machinery of the West. He had even employed motorcars. Few of his supporters had gone to the poll in these vehicles, but, thanks to the intelligent driving of his chauffeurs, many of his opponents had gone to their graves or to the local hospitals, or otherwise abstained from voting. And then something unlooked-for happened. The rival candidate, Ali the Blest, arrived on the scene with his wives and womenfolk, who numbered, roughly, six hundred. Ali had wasted little effort on election literature, but had been heard to remark that every vote given to his opponent meant another sack thrown into the Bosphorus. The Young Turkish candidate, who had conformed to the Western custom of one wife and hardly any mistresses, stood by helplessly while his adversary's poll swelled to a triumphant majority.

"Cristabel Columbus!" he exclaimed, invoking in some confusion the name of a distinguished pioneer; "who would have thought it?"

"Strange," mused Ali, "that one who harangued so clamorously about the Secret Ballot should have overlooked the Veiled Vote."

And, walking homeward with his constituents, he murmured in his beard an improvisation on the heretic poet of Persia:[138]

> "One, rich in metaphors, his Cause contrives
> To urge with edged words, like Kabul knives;
> And I, who worst him in this sorry game,
> Was never rich in anything but—wives."

Judkin Of The Parcels

A figure in an indefinite tweed suit, carrying brown-paper parcels. That is what we met suddenly, at the bend of a muddy Dorsetshire lane, and the roan mare stared and obviously thought of a curtsey. The mare is road-shy, with intervals of stolidity, and there is no telling what she will pass and what she

---

[138] Omar Khayyám again. See introduction.

won't. We call her Redford.[139] That was my first meeting with Judkin, and the next time the circumstances were the same; the same muddy lane, the same rather apologetic figure in the tweed suit, the same—or very similar—parcels. Only this time the roan looked straight in front of her.

Whether I asked the groom or whether he advanced the information, I forget; but someway I gradually reconstructed the life-history of this trudger of the lanes. It was much the same, no doubt, as that of many others who are from time to time pointed out to one as having been aforetime in crack cavalry regiments and noted performers in the saddle; men who have breathed into their lungs the wonder of the East, have romped through life as through a cotillon, have had a thrust perhaps at the Viceroy's Cup, and done fantastic horsefleshy things around the Gulf of Aden. And then a golden stream has dried up, the sunlight has faded suddenly out of things, and the gods have nodded "Go." And they have not gone. They have turned instead to the muddy lanes and cheap villas and the marked-down ills of life, to watch pear trees growing and to encourage hens for their eggs. And Judkin was even as these others; the wine had been suddenly spilt from his cup of life, and he had stayed to suck at the dregs which the wise throw away. In the days of his scorn for most things he would have stared the roan mare and her turn-out out of all pretension to smartness, as he would have frozen a cheap claret behind its cork, or a plain woman behind her veil; and now he was walking stoically through the mud, in a tweed suit that would eventually go on to the gardener's boy, and would perhaps fit him. The dear gods, who know the end before the beginning, were perhaps growing a gardener's boy somewhere to fit the garments, and Judkin was only a caretaker, inhabiting a portion of them. That is what I like to think, and I am probably wrong. And Judkin, whose clothes had been to him once more than a religion, scarcely less sacred than a family quarrel, would

---

[139] Referring to George A. Redford (1847?-1916), the Lord Chamberlain's Examiner of Plays, i.e. the official theatrical censor. Redford was a banker by trade with no real knowledge of the arts and his small-minded and erratic decisions were much criticised by proponents of modern drama.

carry those parcels back to his villa and to the wife who awaited him and them—a wife who may, for all we know to the contrary, have had a figure once, and perhaps has yet a heart of gold—of nine-carat gold, let us say at the least—but assuredly a soul of tape. And he that has fetched and carried will explain how it has fared with him in his dealings, and if he has brought the wrong sort of sugar or thread he will wheedle away the displeasure from that leaden face as a pastrycook girl will drive bluebottles off a stale bun. And that man has known what it was to coax the fret of a thoroughbred, to soothe its toss and sweat as it danced beneath him in the glee and chafe of its pulses and the glory of its thews. He has been in the raw places of the earth, where the desert beasts have whimpered their unthinkable psalmody, and their eyes have shone back the reflex of the midnight stars—and he can immerse himself in the tending of an incubator. It is horrible and wrong, and yet when I have met him in the lanes his face has worn a look of tedious cheerfulness that might pass for happiness. Has Judkin of the Parcels found something in the lees of life that I have missed in going to and fro over many waters? Is there more wisdom in his perverseness than in the madness of the wise? The dear gods know.

I don't think I saw Judkin more than three times all told, and always the lane was our point of contact; but as the roan mare was taking me to the station one heavy, cloud-smeared day, I passed a dull-looking villa that the groom, or instinct, told me was Judkin's home. From beyond a hedge of ragged elder-bushes could be heard the thud, thud of a spade, with an occasional clink and pause, as if some one had picked out a stone and thrown it to a distance, and I knew that *he* was doing nameless things to the roots of a pear tree. Near by him, I felt sure, would be lying a large and late vegetable marrow, and its largeness and lateness would be a theme of conversation at luncheon. It would be suggested that it should grace the harvest thanksgiving service; the harvest having been so generally unsatisfactory, it would be unfair to let the farmers supply all the material for rejoicing.

And while I was speeding townwards along the rails Judkin would be plodding his way to the vicarage bearing a vegetable marrow and a basketful of dahlias. The basket to be returned.

Gabriel-Ernest

"There is a wild beast in your woods," said the artist Cunningham, as he was being driven to the station. It was the only remark he had made during the drive, but as Van Cheele had talked incessantly his companion's silence had not been noticeable.

"A stray fox or two and some resident weasels. Nothing more formidable," said Van Cheele. The artist said nothing.

"What did you mean about a wild beast?" said Van Cheele later, when they were on the platform.

"Nothing. My imagination. Here is the train," said Cunningham.

That afternoon Van Cheele went for one of his frequent rambles through his woodland property. He had a stuffed bittern in his study, and knew the names of quite a number of wild flowers, so his aunt had possibly some justification in describing him as a great naturalist. At any rate, he was a great walker. It was his custom to take mental notes of everything he saw during his walks, not so much for the purpose of assisting contemporary science as to provide topics for conversation afterwards. When the bluebells began to show themselves in flower he made a point of informing every one of the fact; the season of the year might have warned his hearers of the likelihood of such an occurrence, but at least they felt that he was being absolutely frank with them.

What Van Cheele saw on this particular afternoon was, however, something far removed from his ordinary range of experience. On a shelf of smooth stone overhanging a deep pool in the hollow of an oak coppice a boy of about sixteen lay asprawl, drying his wet brown limbs luxuriously in the sun. His wet hair, parted by a recent dive, lay close to his head, and his light-brown eyes, so light that there was an almost tigerish gleam in them, were turned towards Van Cheele with a certain lazy watchfulness. It was an unexpected apparition, and Van Cheele found himself engaged in the novel process of thinking before he spoke. Where on earth could this wild-looking boy hail from? The miller's wife had lost a child some two months ago, supposed to have been swept away by the mill-race, but that had been a mere baby, not a half-grown lad.

"What are you doing there?" he demanded.

"Obviously, sunning myself," replied the boy.

"Where do you live?"

"Here, in these woods."

"You can't live in the woods," said Van Cheele.

"They are very nice woods," said the boy, with a touch of patronage in his voice.

"But where do you sleep at night?"

"I don't sleep at night; that's my busiest time."

Van Cheele began to have an irritated feeling that he was grappling with a problem that was eluding him.

"What do you feed on?" he asked.

"Flesh," said the boy, and he pronounced the word with slow relish, as though he were tasting it.

"Flesh! What Flesh?"

"Since it interests you, rabbits, wild-fowl, hares, poultry, lambs in their season, children when I can get any; they're usually too well locked in at night, when I do most of my hunting. It's quite two months since I tasted child-flesh."

Ignoring the chaffing nature of the last remark Van Cheele tried to draw the boy on the subject of possible poaching operations.

"You're talking rather through your hat when you speak of feeding on hares." (Considering the nature of the boy's toilet the simile was hardly an apt one.) "Our hillside hares aren't easily caught."

"At night I hunt on four feet," was the somewhat cryptic response.

"I suppose you mean that you hunt with a dog?" hazarded Van Cheele.

The boy rolled slowly over on to his back, and laughed a weird low laugh, that was pleasantly like a chuckle and disagreeably like a snarl.

"I don't fancy any dog would be very anxious for my company, especially at night."

Van Cheele began to feel that there was something positively uncanny about the strange-eyed, strange-tongued youngster.

"I can't have you staying in these woods," he declared authoritatively.

"I fancy you'd rather have me here than in your house," said the boy.

The prospect of this wild, nude animal in Van Cheele's primly ordered house was certainly an alarming one.

"If you don't go, I shall have to make you," said Van Cheele.

The boy turned like a flash, plunged into the pool, and in a moment had flung his wet and glistening body half-way up the bank where Van Cheele was standing. In an otter the movement would not have been remarkable; in a boy Van Cheele found it sufficiently startling. His foot slipped as he made an involuntarily backward movement, and he found himself almost prostrate on the slippery weed-grown bank, with those tigerish yellow eyes not very far from his own. Almost instinctively he half raised his hand to his throat. They boy laughed again, a laugh in which the snarl had nearly driven out the chuckle, and then, with another of his astonishing lightning movements, plunged out of view into a yielding tangle of weed and fern.

"What an extraordinary wild animal!" said Van Cheele as he picked himself up. And then he recalled Cunningham's remark "There is a wild beast in your woods."

Walking slowly homeward, Van Cheele began to turn over in his mind various local occurrences which might be traceable to the existence of this astonishing young savage.

Something had been thinning the game in the woods lately, poultry had been missing from the farms, hares were growing unaccountably scarcer, and complaints had reached him of lambs being carried off bodily from the hills. Was it possible that this wild boy was really hunting the countryside in company with some clever poacher dogs? He had spoken of hunting "four-footed" by night, but then, again, he had hinted strangely at no dog caring to come near him, "especially at night." It was certainly puzzling. And then, as Van Cheele ran his mind over the various depredations that had been committed during the last month or two, he came suddenly to a dead stop, alike in his walk and his speculations. The child missing from the mill two months ago—the accepted theory was that it had tumbled into the mill-race and been swept away; but the mother had always declared she had heard a shriek on the hill side of the house, in the opposite direction from the water. It was unthinkable, of course, but he wished that the boy had not made that uncanny remark about child-flesh eaten two months ago. Such dreadful things should not be said even in fun.

Van Cheele, contrary to his usual wont, did not feel disposed to be communicative about his discovery in the wood. His position as a parish councillor and justice of the peace seemed somehow compromised by the fact that he was harbouring a personality of such doubtful repute on his property; there was even a possibility that a heavy bill of damages for raided lambs and poultry might be laid at his door. At dinner that night he was quite unusually silent.

"Where's your voice gone to?" said his aunt. "One would think you had seen a wolf."

Van Cheele, who was not familiar with the old saying, thought the remark rather foolish; if he *had* seen a wolf on his property his tongue would have been extraordinarily busy with the subject.

At breakfast next morning Van Cheele was conscious that his feeling of uneasiness regarding yesterday's episode had not wholly disappeared, and he resolved to go by train to the neighbouring cathedral town, hunt up Cunningham, and learn from him what he had really seen that had prompted the remark about a wild beast in the woods. With this resolution taken, his usual cheerfulness partially returned, and he hummed a bright little melody as he sauntered to the morning-room for his customary cigarette. As he entered the room the melody made way abruptly for a pious invocation. Gracefully asprawl on the ottoman, in an attitude of almost exaggerated repose, was the boy of the woods. He was drier than when Van Cheele had last seen him, but no other alteration was noticeable in his toilet.

"How dare you come here?" asked Van Cheele furiously.

"You told me I was not to stay in the woods," said the boy calmly.

"But not to come here. Supposing my aunt should see you!"

And with a view to minimising that catastrophe, Van Cheele hastily obscured as much of his unwelcome guest as possible under the folds of a *Morning Post*. At that moment his aunt entered the room.

"This is a poor boy who has lost his way—and lost his memory. He doesn't know who he is or where he comes from," explained Van Cheele desperately, glancing apprehensively at the waif's face to see whether he was going to add inconvenient candour to his other savage propensities.

Miss Van Cheele was enormously interested.

"Perhaps his underlinen is marked," she suggested.

"He seems to have lost most of that, too," said Van Cheele, making frantic little grabs at the *Morning Post* to keep it in its place.

A naked homeless child appealed to Miss Van Cheele as warmly as a stray kitten or derelict puppy would have done.

"We must do all we can for him," she decided, and in a very short time a messenger, dispatched to the rectory, where a pageboy was kept, had returned with a suit of pantry clothes, and the necessary accessories of shirt, shoes, collar, etc. Clothed, clean, and groomed, the boy lost none of his uncanniness in Van Cheele's eyes, but his aunt found him sweet.

"We must call him something till we know who he really is," she said. "Gabriel-Ernest, I think; those are nice suitable names."

Van Cheele agreed, but he privately doubted whether they were being grafted on to a nice suitable child. His misgivings were not diminished by the fact that his staid and elderly spaniel had bolted out of the house at the first incoming of the boy, and now obstinately remained shivering and yapping at the farther end of the orchard, while the canary, usually as vocally industrious as Van Cheele himself, had put itself on an allowance of frightened cheeps. More than ever he was resolved to consult Cunningham without loss of time.

As he drove off to the station his aunt was arranging that Gabriel-Ernest should help her to entertain the infant members of her Sunday-school class at tea that afternoon.

Cunningham was not at first disposed to be communicative.

"My mother died of some brain trouble," he explained, "so you will understand why I am averse to dwelling on anything of an impossibly fantastic nature that I may see or think that I have seen."

"But what *did* you see?" persisted Van Cheele.

"What I thought I saw was something so extraordinary that no really sane man could dignify it with the credit of having actually happened. I was standing, the last evening I was with you, half-hidden in the hedgegrowth by the orchard gate, watching the dying glow of the sunset. Suddenly I became aware of a naked boy, a bather from some neighbouring pool, I took him to be, who was standing out on the bare hillside also watching the sunset. His pose was so suggestive of some wild faun of Pagan myth that I instantly wanted to engage him as a model, and in another moment I think I should have hailed him. But just then the sun dipped out of view, and all the orange and pink slid out of the landscape, leaving it cold and grey. And at the same moment an astounding thing happened—the boy vanished too!"

"What! vanished away into nothing?" asked Van Cheele excitedly.

"No; that is the dreadful part of it," answered the artist; "on the open hillside where the boy had been standing a second ago, stood a large wolf, blackish in colour, with gleaming fangs and cruel, yellow eyes. You may think— "

But Van Cheele did not stop for anything as futile as thought. Already he was tearing at top speed towards the station. He dismissed the idea of a telegram. "Gabriel-Ernest is a werewolf" was a hopelessly inadequate effort at conveying the situation, and his aunt would think it was a code message to which he had omitted to give her the key. His one hope was that he might reach home before sundown. The cab which he chartered at the other end of the railway journey bore him with what seemed exasperating slowness along the country roads, which were pink and mauve with the flush of the sinking sun. His aunt was putting away some unfinished jams and cake when he arrived.

"Where is Gabriel-Ernest?" he almost screamed.

"He is taking the little Toop child home," said his aunt. "It was getting so late, I thought it wasn't safe to let it go back alone. What a lovely sunset, isn't it?"

But Van Cheele, although not oblivious of the glow in the western sky, did not stay to discuss its beauties. At a speed for which he was scarcely geared he raced along the narrow lane that led to the home of the Toops. On one side ran the swift current of the mill-stream, on the other rose the stretch of bare hillside. A dwindling rim of red sun showed still on the skyline, and the next turning must bring him in view of the ill-assorted couple he was pursuing. Then the colour went suddenly out of things, and a grey light settled itself with a quick shiver over the landscape. Van Cheele heard a shrill wail of fear, and stopped running.

Nothing was ever seen again of the Toop child or Gabriel-Ernest, but the latter's discarded garments were found lying in the road so it was assumed that the child had fallen into the water, and that the boy had stripped and jumped in, in a vain endeavour to save it. Van Cheele and some workmen who were near by at the time testified to having heard a child scream loudly just near the spot where the clothes were found. Mrs. Toop, who had eleven other children, was decently resigned to her bereavement, but Miss Van Cheele sincerely mourned her lost foundling. It was on her initiative that a memorial brass was put up in the parish church to "Gabriel-Ernest, an unknown boy, who bravely sacrificed his life for another."

Van Cheele gave way to his aunt in most things, but he flatly refused to subscribe to the Gabriel-Ernest memorial.

The Saint And The Goblin

The little stone Saint occupied a retired niche in a side aisle of the old cathedral. No one quite remembered who he had been, but that in a way was a guarantee of respectability. At least so the Goblin said. The Goblin was a very fine specimen of quaint stone carving, and lived up in the corbel on the wall opposite the niche of the little Saint. He was connected with some of the best cathedral folk, such as the queer carvings in the choir stalls and chancel screen, and even the gargoyles high up on the roof. All the fantastic beasts and manikins that sprawled and twisted in wood or stone or lead overhead in the arches or away down in the crypt were in some way akin to him; consequently he was a person of recognised importance in the cathedral world.

The little stone Saint and the Goblin got on very well together, though they looked at most things from different points of view. The Saint was a philanthropist in an old fashioned way; he thought the world, as he saw it, was good, but might be improved. In particular he pitied the church mice, who were miserably poor. The Goblin, on the other hand, was of opinion that the world, as he knew it, was bad, but had better be let alone. It was the function of the church mice to be poor.

"All the same," said the Saint, "I feel very sorry for them."

"Of course you do," said the Goblin; "it's *your* function to feel sorry for them. If they were to leave off being poor you couldn't fulfil your functions. You'd be a sinecure."

He rather hoped that the Saint would ask him what a sinecure meant, but the latter took refuge in a stony silence. The Goblin might be right, but still, he thought, he would like to do something for the church mice before winter came on; they were so very poor.

Whilst he was thinking the matter over he was startled by something falling between his feet with a hard metallic clatter. It was a bright new thaler; one of the cathedral jackdaws, who collected such things, had flown in with it to a stone cornice just above his niche, and the banging of the sacristy door had star-

THE SAINT AND THE GOBLIN

tled him into dropping it. Since the invention of gunpowder the family nerves were not what they had been.

"What have you got there?" asked the Goblin.

"A silver thaler," said the Saint. "Really," he continued, "it is most fortunate; now I can do something for the church mice."

"How will you manage it?" asked the Goblin.

The Saint considered.

"I will appear in a vision to the vergeress who sweeps the floors. I will tell her that she will find a silver thaler between my feet, and that she must take it and buy a measure of corn and put it on my shrine. When she finds the money she will know that it was a true dream, and she will take care to follow my directions. Then the mice will have food all the winter."

"Of course *you* can do that," observed the Goblin. "Now, I can only appear to people after they have had a heavy supper of indigestible things. My opportunities with the vergeress would be limited. There is some advantage in being a saint after all."

All this while the coin was lying at the Saint's feet. It was clean and glittering and had the Elector's arms beautifully stamped upon it. The Saint began to reflect that such an opportunity was too rare to be hastily disposed of. Perhaps indiscriminate charity might be harmful to the church mice. After all, it was their function to be poor; the Goblin had said so, and the Goblin was generally right.

"I've been thinking," he said to that personage, "that perhaps it would be really better if I ordered a thaler's worth of candles to be placed on my shrine instead of the corn."

He often wished, for the look of the thing, that people would sometimes burn candles at his shrine; but as they had forgotten who he was it was not considered a profitable speculation to pay him that attention.

"Candles would be more orthodox," said the Goblin.

"More orthodox, certainly," agreed the Saint, "and the mice could have the ends to eat; candle-ends are most fattening."

The Goblin was too well bred to wink; besides, being a stone goblin, it was out of the question.

"Well, if it ain't there, sure enough!" said the vergeress next morning. She took the shining coin down from the dusty niche and turned it over and over in her grimy hands. Then she put it to her mouth and bit it.

"She can't be going to eat it," thought the Saint, and fixed her with his stoniest stare.

"Well," said the woman, in a somewhat shriller key, "who'd have thought it! A saint, too!"

Then she did an unaccountable thing. She hunted an old piece of tape out of her pocket, and tied it crosswise, with a big loop, round the thaler, and hung it round the neck of the little Saint.

Then she went away.

"The only possible explanation," said the Goblin, "is that it's a bad one."

* * *

"What is that decoration your neighbour is wearing?" asked a wyvern[140] that was wrought into the capital of an adjacent pillar.

The Saint was ready to cry with mortification, only, being of stone, he couldn't.

"It's a coin of—ahem!—fabulous value," replied the Goblin tactfully.

And the news went round the Cathedral that the shrine of the little stone Saint had been enriched by a priceless offering.

"After all, it's something to have the conscience of a goblin," said the Saint to himself.

The church mice were as poor as ever. But that was their function.

The Soul of Laploshka

Laploshka was one of the meanest men I have ever met, and quite one of the most entertaining. He said horrid things about other people in such a charming way that one forgave him for the equally horrid things he said about oneself behind one's back.

---
[140] A dragon-like creature with two legs and wings.

THE SOUL OF LAPLOSHKA

Hating anything in the way of ill-natured gossip ourselves, we are always grateful to those who do it for us and do it well. And Laploshka did it really well.

Naturally Laploshka had a large circle of acquaintances, and as he exercised some care in their selection it followed that an appreciable proportion were men whose bank balances enabled them to acquiesce indulgently in his rather one-sided views on hospitality. Thus, although possessed of only moderate means, he was able to live comfortably within his income, and still more comfortably within those of various tolerantly disposed associates.

But towards the poor or to those of the same limited resources as himself his attitude was one of watchful anxiety; he seemed to be haunted by a besetting fear lest some fraction of a shilling or franc, or whatever the prevailing coinage might be, should be diverted from his pocket or service into that of a hard-up companion. A two-franc cigar would be cheerfully offered to a wealthy patron, on the principle of doing evil that good may come, but I have known him indulge in agonies of perjury rather than admit the incriminating possession of a copper coin when change was needed to tip a waiter. The coin would have been duly returned at the earliest opportunity—he would have taken means to insure against forgetfulness on the part of the borrower—but accidents might happen, and even the temporary estrangement from his penny or sou was a calamity to be avoided.

The knowledge of this amiable weakness offered a perpetual temptation to play upon Laploshka's fears of involuntary generosity. To offer him a lift in a cab and pretend not to have enough money to pay the fair, to fluster him with a request for a sixpence when his hand was full of silver just received in change, these were a few of the petty torments that ingenuity prompted as occasion afforded. To do justice to Laploshka's resourcefulness it must be admitted that he always emerged somehow or other from the most embarrassing dilemma without in any way compromising his reputation for saying "No." But the gods send opportunities at some time to most men, and mine came one evening when Laploshka and I were supping together in a cheap boulevard restaurant. (Except when he was the bidden guest of some one with an irreproachable income, Laploshka was wont to curb his appetite for high living; on such fortunate occasions he let it go on an easy snaffle.)[141] At the conclusion of the meal a somewhat urgent message called me away, and without heeding my companion's agitated protest, I called back cruelly, "Pay my share; I'll settle with you to-morrow." Early on the morrow Laploshka hunted me down by instinct as I walked along a side street that I hardly ever frequented. He had the air of a man who had not slept.

"You owe me two francs from last night," was his breathless greeting.

I spoke evasively of the situation in Portugal, where more trouble seemed brewing. But Laploshka listened with the abstraction of the deaf adder, and quickly returned to the subject of the two francs.

"I'm afraid I must owe it to you," I said lightly and brutally. "I haven't a sou in the world," and I added mendaciously, "I'm going away for six months or perhaps longer."

Laploshka said nothing, but his eyes bulged a little and his cheeks took on the mottled hues of an ethnographical map of the Balkan Peninsula. That same day, at sundown, he died. "Failure of the heart's action," was the doctor's verdict; but I, who knew better, knew that he died of grief.

There arose the problem of what to do with his two francs. To have killed Laploshka was one thing; to have kept his beloved money would have argued a callousness of feeling of which I am not capable. The ordinary solution, of giving it to the poor, would by no means fit the present situation, for nothing would have distressed the dead man more than such a misuse of his property. On the other hand, the bestowal of two francs on the rich was an operation which called for some tact. An easy way out of the difficulty seemed, however, to present itself the following Sunday, as I was wedged into the cosmopolitan crowd which

---

[141] A snaffle is a type of bit on a horse's bridle.

filled the side-aisle of one of the most popular Paris churches. A collecting-bag, for "the poor of Monsieur le Curé," was buffeting its tortuous way across the seemingly impenetrable human sea, and a German in front of me, who evidently did not wish his appreciation of the magnificent music to be marred by a suggestion of payment, made audible criticisms to his companion on the claims of the said charity.

"They do not want money," he said; "they have too much money. They have no poor. They are all pampered."

If that were really the case my way seemed clear. I dropped Laploshka's two francs into the bag with a murmured blessing on the rich of Monsieur le Curé.

Some three weeks later chance had taken me to Vienna, and I sat one evening regaling myself in a humble but excellent little Gasthaus up in the Währinger quarter.[142] The appointments were primitive, but the Schnitzel, the beer, and the cheese could not have been improved on. Good cheer brought good custom, and with the exception of one small table near the door every place was occupied. Half-way through my meal I happened to glance in the direction of that empty seat, and saw that it was no longer empty. Poring over the bill of fare with the absorbed scrutiny of one who seeks the cheapest among the cheap was Laploshka. Once he looked across at me, with a comprehensive glance at my repast, as though to say, "It is my two francs you are eating," and then looked swiftly away. Evidently the poor of Monsieur le Curé had been genuine poor. The Schnitzel turned to leather in my mouth, the beer seemed tepid; I left the Emmenthaler untasted. My one idea was to get away from the room, away from the table where *that* was seated; and as I fled I felt Laploshka's reproachful eyes watching the amount that I gave to the piccolo[143]—out of his two francs. I lunched next day at an expensive restaurant which I felt sure that the living Laploshka would never have entered on his own account, and I hoped that the dead Laploshka would observe the same barriers. I was not

---

[142] In the north-west of the city.

[143] A young or apprentice waiter.

mistaken, but as I came out I found him miserably studying the bill of fare stuck up on the portals. Then he slowly made his way over to a milk-hall.[144] For the first time in my experience I missed the charm and gaiety of Vienna life.

After that, in Paris or London or wherever I happened to be, I continued to see a good deal of Laploshka. If I had a seat in a box at a theatre I was always conscious of his eyes furtively watching me from the dim recesses of the gallery. As I turned into my club on a rainy afternoon I would see him taking inadequate shelter in a doorway opposite. Even if I indulged in the modest luxury of a penny chair in the Park he generally confronted me from one of the free benches, never staring at me, but always elaborately conscious of my presence. My friends began to comment on my changed looks, and advised me to leave off heaps of things. I should have liked to have left off Laploshka.

On a certain Sunday—it was probably Easter, for the crush was worse than ever—I was again wedged into the crowd listening to the music in the fashionable Paris church, and again the collection-bag was buffeting its way across the human sea. An English lady behind me was making ineffectual efforts to convey a coin into the still distant bag, so I took the money at her request and helped it forward to its destination. It was a two-franc piece. A swift inspiration came to me, and I merely dropped my own sou into the bag and slid the silver coin into my pocket. I had withdrawn Laploshka's two francs from the poor, who should never have had the legacy. As I backed away from the crowd I heard a woman's voice say, "I don't believe he put my money in the bag. There are swarms of people in Paris like that!" But my mind was lighter that it had been for a long time.

The delicate mission of bestowing the retrieved sum on the deserving rich still confronted me. Again I trusted to the inspiration of accident, and again fortune favoured me. A shower drove me, two days later, into one of the historic churches on the left bank of the Seine, and there I found, peering at the old woodcarvings, the Baron R., one of the wealthiest and most shabbily

---

[144] A hall where fresh, unpasteurised milk was sold for consumption.

dressed men in Paris. It was now or never. Putting a strong American inflection into the French which I usually talked with an unmistakable British accent, I catechised the Baron as to the date of the church's building, its dimensions, and other details which an American tourist would be certain to want to know. Having acquired such information as the Baron was able to impart on short notice, I solemnly placed the two-franc piece in his hand, with the hearty assurance that it was "pour vous," and turned to go. The Baron was slightly taken aback, but accepted the situation with a good grace. Walking over to a small box fixed in the wall, he dropped Laploshka's two francs into the slot. Over the box was the inscription, "Pour les pauvres de M. le Curé."[145]

That evening, at the crowded corner by the Café de la Paix,[146] I caught a fleeting glimpse of Laploshka. He smiled, slightly raised his hat, and vanished. I never saw him again. After all, the money had been *given* to the deserving rich, and the soul of Laploshka was at peace.

The Bag

"The Major is coming in to tea," said Mrs. Hoopington to her niece. "He's just gone round to the stables with his horse. Be as bright and lively as you can; the poor man's got a fit of the glooms."

Major Pallaby was a victim of circumstances, over which he had no control, and of his temper, over which he had very little. He had taken on the Mastership of the Pexdale Hounds in succession to a highly popular man who had fallen foul of his committee, and the Major found himself confronted with the overt hostility of at least half the hunt, while his lack of tact and amiability had done much to alienate the remainder. Hence subscriptions were beginning to fall off, foxes grew provokingly scarcer,

---
[145] (French) "For the poor of the curate".
[146] One of Paris' grandest cafés, near the Opéra, in the 9th arrondissement.

and wire obtruded itself with increasing frequency. The Major could plead reasonable excuse for his fit of the glooms.

In ranging herself as a partisan on the side of Major Pallaby Mrs. Hoopington had been largely influenced by the fact that she had made up her mind to marry him at an early date. Against his notorious bad temper she set his three thousand a year, and his prospective succession to a baronetcy gave a casting vote in his favour. The Major's plans on the subject of matrimony were not at present in such an advanced stage as Mrs. Hoopington's, but he was beginning to find his way over to Hoopington Hall with a frequency that was already being commented on.

"He had a wretchedly thin field out again yesterday," said Mrs. Hoopington. "Why you didn't bring one or two hunting men down with you, instead of that stupid Russian boy, I can't think."

"Vladimir isn't stupid," protested her niece; "he's one of the most amusing boys I ever met. Just compare him for a moment with some of your heavy hunting men—"

"Anyhow, my dear Norah, he can't ride."

"Russians never can; but he shoots."

"Yes; and what does he shoot? Yesterday he brought home a woodpecker in his game-bag."

"But he'd shot three pheasants and some rabbits as well."

"That's no excuse for including a woodpecker in his game-bag."

"Foreigners go in for mixed bags more than we do. A Grand Duke pots a vulture just as seriously as we should stalk a bustard. Anyhow, I've explained to Vladimir that certain birds are beneath his dignity as a sportsman. And as he's only nineteen, of course, his dignity is a sure thing to appeal to."

Mrs. Hoopington sniffed. Most people with whom Vladimir came in contact found his high spirits infectious, but his present hostess was guaranteed immune against infection of that sort.

"I hear him coming in now," she observed. "I shall go and get ready for tea. We're going to have it here in the hall. Entertain the Major if he comes in before I'm down, and, above all, be bright."

THE BAG

Norah was dependent on her aunt's good graces for many little things that made life worth living, and she was conscious of a feeling of discomfiture because the Russian youth whom she had brought down as a welcome element of change in the country-house routine was not making a good impression. That young gentleman, however, was supremely unconscious of any shortcomings, and burst into the hall, tired, and less sprucely groomed than usual, but distinctly radiant. His game-bag looked comfortably full.

"Guess what I have shot," he demanded.

"Pheasants, wood-pigeons, rabbits," hazarded Norah.

"No; a large beast; I don't know what you call it in English. Brown, with a darkish tail." Norah changed colour.

"Does it live in a tree and eat nuts?" she asked, hoping that the use of the adjective "large" might be an exaggeration.

Vladimir laughed.

"Oh no; not a *biyelka*."

"Does it swim and eat fish?" asked Norah, with a fervent prayer in her heart that it might turn out to be an otter.

"No," said Vladimir, busy with the straps of his game-bag; "it lives in the woods, and eats rabbits and chickens."

Norah sat down suddenly, and hid her face in her hands.

"Merciful Heaven!" she wailed; "he's shot a fox!"

Vladimir looked up at her in consternation. In a torrent of agitated words she tried to explain the horror of the situation. The boy understood nothing, but was thoroughly alarmed.

"Hide it, hide it!" said Norah frantically, pointing to the still unopened bag. "My aunt and the Major will be here in a moment. Throw it on the top of that chest; they won't see it there."

Vladimir swung the bag with fair aim; but the strap caught in its flight on the outstanding point of an antler fixed in the wall, and the bag, with its terrible burden, remained suspended just above the alcove where tea would presently be laid. At that moment Mrs. Hoopington and the Major entered the hall.

"The Major is going to draw our covers to-morrow," announced the lady, with a certain heavy satisfaction. "Smithers is confident that we'll be able to show him some sport; he swears he's seen a fox in the nut copse three times this week."

"I'm sure I hope so; I hope so," said the Major moodily. "I must break this sequence of blank days. One hears so often that a fox has settled down as a tenant for life in certain covers, and then when you go to turn him out there isn't a trace of him. I'm certain a fox was shot or trapped in Lady Widden's woods the very day before we drew them."

"Major, if any one tried that game on in my woods they'd get short shrift," said Mrs. Hoopington.

Norah found her way mechanically to the tea-table and made her fingers frantically busy in rearranging the parsley round the sandwich dish. On one side of her loomed the morose countenance of the Major, on the other she was conscious of the scared, miserable eyes of Vladimir. And above it all hung *that*. She dared not raise her eyes above the level of the tea-table, and she almost expected to see a spot of accusing vulpine blood drip down and stain the whiteness of the cloth. Her aunt's manner signalled to her the repeated message to "be bright"; for the present she was fully occupied in keeping her teeth from chattering.

"What did you shoot to-day?" asked Mrs. Hoopington suddenly of the unusually silent Vladimir.

"Nothing—nothing worth speaking of," said the boy.

Norah's heart, which had stood still for a space, made up for lost time with a most disturbing bound.

"I wish you'd find something that was worth speaking about," said the hostess; "every one seems to have lost their tongues."

"When did Smithers last see that fox?" said the Major.

"Yesterday morning; a fine dog-fox, with a dark brush," confided Mrs. Hoopington.

"Aha, we'll have a good gallop after that brush to-morrow," said the Major, with a transient gleam of good humour. And then gloomy silence settled again round the tea-table, a silence broken only by despondent munchings and the occasional feverish rattle of a teaspoon in its saucer. A diversion was at last afforded by Mrs. Hoopington's fox-terrier, which had jumped on to a vacant chair, the better to survey the delicacies of the table, and was now sniffing in an upward direction at something apparently more interesting than cold tea-cake.

"What is exciting him?" asked his mistress, as the dog suddenly broke into short angry barks, with a running accompaniment of tremulous whines.

"Why," she continued, "it's your game-bag, Vladimir! What *have* you got in it?"

"By Gad," said the Major, who was now standing up; "there's a pretty warm scent!"

And then a simultaneous idea flashed on himself and Mrs. Hoopington. Their faces flushed to distinct but harmonious tones of purple, and with one accusing voice they screamed, "You've shot the fox!"

Norah tried hastily to palliate Vladimir's misdeed in their eyes, but it is doubtful whether they heard her. The Major's fury clothed and reclothed itself in words as frantically as a woman up in town for one day's shopping tries on a succession of garments. He reviled and railed at fate and the general scheme of things, he pitied himself with a strong, deep pity too poignant for tears, he condemned every one with whom he had ever come in contact to endless and abnormal punishments. In fact, he conveyed the impression that if a destroying angel had been lent to him for a week it would have had very little time for private study. In the lulls of his outcry could be heard the querulous monotone of Mrs. Hoopington and the sharp staccato barking of the fox-terrier. Vladimir, who did not understand a tithe of what was being said, sat fondling a cigarette and repeating under his breath from time to time a vigorous English adjective which he had long ago taken affectionately into his vocabulary. His mind strayed back to the youth in the old Russian folk-tale who shot an enchanted bird with dramatic results. Meanwhile, the Major, roaming round the hall like an imprisoned cyclone, had caught sight of and joyfully pounced on the telephone apparatus, and lost no time in ringing up the hunt secretary and announcing his resignation of the Mastership. A servant had by this time brought his horse round to the door, and in a few seconds Mrs. Hoopington's shrill monotone had the field to itself. But after the Major's display her best efforts at vocal violence missed their full effect; it was as though one had come straight out from a Wagner opera into a rather tame thunderstorm. Realising, perhaps, that her tirades were something of an anticlimax, Mrs. Hoopington broke suddenly into some rather necessary tears and marched out of the room, leaving behind her a silence almost as terrible as the turmoil which had preceded it.

"What shall I do with—*that*?" asked Vladimir at last.

"Bury it," said Norah.

"Just plain burial?" said Vladimir, rather relieved. He had almost expected that some of the local clergy would have insisted on being present, or that a salute might have to be fired over the grave.

And thus it came to pass that in the dusk of a November evening the Russian boy, murmuring a few of the prayers of his Church for luck, gave hasty but decent burial to a large polecat under the lilac trees at Hoopington.

The Strategist

Mrs. Jallatt's young people's parties were severely exclusive; it came cheaper that way, because you could ask fewer to them. Mrs. Jallatt didn't study cheapness, but somehow she generally attained it.

"There'll be about ten girls," speculated Rollo, as he drove to the function, "and I suppose four fellows, unless the Wrotsleys bring their cousin, which Heaven forbid. That would mean Jack and me against three of them."

Rollo and the Wrotsley brethren had maintained an undying feud almost from nursery days. They only met now and then in the holidays, and the meeting was usually tragic for whichever happened to have the fewest backers on hand. Rollo was counting to-night on the presence of a devoted and muscular partisan to hold an even balance. As he arrived he heard his prospective champion's sister apologising to the hostess for the unavoidable absence of her brother; a moment later he noted that the Wrotsleys *had* brought their cousin.

Two against three would have been exciting and possibly unpleasant; one against three promised to be about as amusing as a visit to the dentist. Rollo ordered his carriage for as early as was decently possible, and faced the company with a smile that he imagined the better sort of aristocrat would have worn when mounting to the guillotine.

"So glad you were able to come," said the elder Wrotsley heartily.

"Now, you children will like to play games, I suppose," said Mrs. Jallatt, by way of giving things a start, and as they were too well-bred to contradict her there only remained the question of what they were to play at.

"I know of a good game," said the elder Wrotsley innocently. "The fellows leave the room and think of a word; then they come back again, and the girls have to find out what the word is."

Rollo knew the game. He would have suggested it himself if his faction had been in the majority.

"It doesn't promise to be very exciting," sniffed the superior Dolores Sneep as the boys filed out of the room. Rollo thought differently. He trusted to Providence that Wrotsley had nothing worse than knotted handkerchiefs at his disposal.

The word-choosers locked themselves in the library to ensure that their deliberations should not be interrupted. Providence turned out to be not even decently neutral; on a rack on the library wall were a dog-whip and a whalebone riding-switch. Rollo thought it criminal negligence to leave such weapons of precision lying about. He was given a choice of evils, and chose the dog-whip; the next minute or so he spent in wondering how he could have made such a stupid selection. Then they went back to the languidly expectant females.

"The word's 'camel,'" announced the Wrotsley cousin blunderingly.

"You stupid!" screamed the girls, "we've got to *guess* the word. Now you'll have to go back and think of another."

"Not for worlds," said Rollo; "I mean, the word isn't really camel; we were rotting. Pretend it's dromedary!" he whispered to the others.

"I heard them say 'dromedary'! I heard them. I don't care what you say; I heard them," squealed the odious Dolores. "With ears as long as hers one would hear anything," thought Rollo savagely.

"We shall have to go back, I suppose," said the elder Wrotsley resignedly.

The conclave locked itself once more into the library. "Look here, I'm not going through that dog-whip business again," protested Rollo.

"Certainly not, dear," said the elder Wrotsley; "we'll try the whalebone switch this time, and you'll know which hurts most. It's only by personal experience that one finds out these things."

It was swiftly borne in upon Rollo that his earlier selection of the dog-whip had been a really sound one. The conclave gave his under-lip time to steady itself while it debated the choice of the necessary word. "Mustang" was no good, as half the girls wouldn't know what it meant; finally "quagga" was pitched on.

"You must come and sit down over here," chorused the investigating committee on their return; but Rollo was obdurate in insisting that the questioned person always stood up. On the whole, it was a relief when the game was ended and supper was announced.

Mrs. Jallatt did not stint her young guests, but the more expensive delicacies of her supper-table were never unnecessarily duplicated, and it was usually good policy to take what you wanted while it was still there. On this occasion she had provided sixteen peaches to "go round" among fourteen children; it was really not her fault that the two Wrotsleys and their cousin, foreseeing the long foodless drive home, had each quietly pocketed an extra peach, but it was distinctly trying for Dolores and the fat and good-natured Agnes Blaik to be left with one peach between them.

"I suppose we had better halve it," said Dolores sourly.

But Agnes was fat first and good-natured afterwards; those were her guiding principles in life. She was profuse in her sympathy for Dolores, but she hastily devoured the peach, explaining that it would spoil it to divide it; the juice ran out so.

"Now what would you all like to do?" demanded Mrs. Jallatt by way of diversion. "The professional conjurer whom I had engaged has failed me at the last moment. Can any of you recite?"

There were symptoms of a general panic. Dolores was known to recite "Locksley Hall"[147] on the least provocation. There had been occasions when her opening line, "Comrades, leave me here a little," had been taken as a literal injunction by a large section of her hearers. There was a murmur of relief when Rollo hastily declared that he could do a few conjuring tricks. He had never done one in his life, but those two visits to the library had goaded him to unusual recklessness.

"You've seen conjuring chaps take coins and cards out of people," he announced; "well, I'm going to take more interesting things out of some of you. Mice, for instance."

"Not mice!"

A shrill protest rose, as he had foreseen, from the majority of his audience.

"Well, fruit, them."

The amended proposal was received with approval. Agnes positively beamed.

Without more ado Rollo made straight for his trio of enemies, plunged his hand successively into their breast-pockets, and produced three peaches. There was no applause, but no amount of hand-clapping would have given the performer as much pleasure as the silence which greeted his coup.

"Of course, we were in the know," said the Wrotsley cousin lamely.

"That's done it," chuckled Rollo to himself.

"If they *had* been confederates they would have sworn they knew nothing about it," said Dolores, with piercing conviction.

---

[147] A dramatic monologue in verse, written in 1835 and published in 1842, by Alfred, Lord Tennyson.

"Do you know any more tricks?" asked Mrs. Jallatt hurriedly.

Rollo did not. He hinted that he might have changed the three peaches into something else, but Agnes had already converted one into girl-food, so nothing more could be done in that direction.

"I know a game," said the elder Wrotsley heavily, "where the fellows go out of the room, and think of some character in history; then they come back and act him, and the girls have to guess who it's meant for."

"I'm afraid I must be going," said Rollo to his hostess.

"Your carriage won't be here for another twenty minutes," said Mrs. Jallatt.

"It's such a fine evening I think I'll walk and meet it."

"It's raining rather steadily at present. You've just time to play that historical game."

"We haven't heard Dolores recite," said Rollo desperately; as soon as he had said it he realised his mistake. Confronted with the alternative of "Locksley Hall," public opinion declared unanimously for the history game.

Rollo played his last card. In an undertone meant apparently for the Wrotsley boy, but carefully pitched to reach Agnes, he observed—

"All right, old man; we'll go and finish those chocolates we left in the library."

"I think it's only fair that the girls should take their turn in going out," exclaimed Agnes briskly. She was great on fairness.

"Nonsense," said the others; "there are too many of us."

"Well, four of us can go. I'll be one of them."

And Agnes darted off towards the library, followed by three less eager damsels.

Rollo sank into a chair and smiled ever so faintly at the Wrotsleys, just a momentary baring of the teeth; an otter, escaping from the fangs of the hounds into the safety of a deep pool, might have given a similar demonstration of feelings.

From the library came the sound of moving furniture. Agnes was leaving nothing unturned in her quest for the mythical chocolates. And then came a more blessed sound, wheels crunching wet gravel.

"It has been a most enjoyable evening," said Rollo to his hostess.

Cross Currents

Vanessa Pennington had a husband who was poor, with few extenuating circumstances, and an admirer who, though comfortably rich, was cumbered with a sense of honour. His wealth made him welcome in Vanessa's eyes, but his code of what was right impelled him to go away and forget her, or at the most to think of her in the intervals of doing a great many other things. And although Alaric Clyde loved Vanessa, and thought he should always go on loving her, he gradually and unconsciously allowed himself to be wooed and won by a more alluring mistress; he fancied that his continued shunning of the haunts of men was a self-imposed exile, but his heart was caught in the spell of the Wilderness, and the Wilderness was kind and beautiful to him. When one is young and strong and unfettered the wild earth can be very kind and very beautiful. Witness the legion of men who were once young and unfettered and now eat out their souls in dustbins, because, having erstwhile known and loved the Wilderness, they broke from her thrall and turned aside into beaten paths.

In the high waste places of the world Clyde roamed and hunted and dreamed, death-dealing and gracious as some god of Hellas, moving with his horses and servants and four-footed camp followers from one dwelling ground to another, a welcome guest among wild primitive village folk and nomads, a friend and slayer of the fleet, shy beasts around him. By the shores of misty upland lakes he shot the wild fowl that had winged their way to him across half the old world; beyond Bokhara[148] he watched the wild Aryan horsemen at their gambols; watched, too, in some dim-lit tea-house one of those beautiful uncouth

---
[148] More commonly Bukhara, an historical city in Uzbekistan.

dances that one can never wholly forget; or, making a wide cast down to the valley of the Tigris, swam and rolled in its snow-cooled racing waters. Vanessa, meanwhile, in a Bayswater back street, was making out the weekly laundry list, attending bargain sales, and, in her more adventurous moments, trying new ways of cooking whiting. Occasionally she went to bridge parties, where, if the play was not illuminating, at least one learned a great deal about the private life of some of the Royal and Imperial Houses. Vanessa, in a way, was glad that Clyde had done the proper thing. She had a strong natural bias towards respectability, though she would have preferred to have been respectable in smarter surroundings, where her example would have done more good. To be beyond reproach was one thing, but it would have been nicer to have been nearer to the Park.[149]

And then of a sudden her regard for respectability and Clyde's sense of what was right were thrown on the scrap-heap of unnecessary things. They had been useful and highly important in their time, but the death of Vanessa's husband made them of no immediate moment.

The news of the altered condition of things followed Clyde with leisurely persistence from one place of call to another, and at last ran him to a standstill somewhere in the Orenburg Steppe.[150] He would have found it exceedingly difficult to analyse his feelings on receipt of the tidings. The Fates had unexpectedly (and perhaps just a little officiously) removed an obstacle from his path. He supposed he was overjoyed, but he missed the feeling of elation which he had experienced some four months ago when he had bagged a snow-leopard with a lucky shot after a day's fruitless stalking. Of course he would go back and ask Vanessa to marry him, but he was determined on enforcing a condition; on no account would he desert his newer love. Vanessa would have to agree to come out into the Wilderness with him.

---

[149]The fashionable Hyde Park area of London.

[150]On the Ural River, near to what today is Kazakhstan.

The lady hailed the return of her lover with even more relief than had been occasioned by his departure. The death of John Pennington had left his widow in circumstances which were more straitened than ever, and the Park had receded even from her notepaper, where it had long been retained as a courtesy title on the principle that addresses are given to us to conceal our whereabouts. Certainly she was more independent now than heretofore, but independence, which means so much to many women, was of little account to Vanessa, who came under the heading of the mere female. She made little ado about accepting Clyde's condition, and announced herself ready to follow him to the end of the world; as the world was round she nourished a complacent idea that in the ordinary course of things one would find oneself in the neighbourhood of Hyde Park Corner sooner or later no matter how far afield one wandered.

East of Budapest her complacency began to filter away, and when she saw her husband treating the Black Sea with a familiarity which she had never been able to assume towards the English Channel, misgivings began to crowd in upon her. Adventures which would have presented an amusing and enticing aspect to a better-bred woman aroused in Vanessa only the twin sensations of fright and discomfort. Flies bit her, and she was persuaded that it was only sheer boredom that prevented camels from doing the same. Clyde did his best, and a very good best it was, to infuse something of the banquet into their prolonged desert picnics, but even snow-cooled Heidsieck[151] lost its flavour when you were convinced that the dusky cupbearer who served it with such reverent elegance was only waiting a convenient opportunity to cut your throat. It was useless for Clyde to give Yussuf a character for devotion such as is rarely found in any Western servant. Vanessa was well enough educated to know that all dusky-skinned people take human life as unconcernedly as Bayswater folk take singing lessons.

And with a growing irritation and querulousness on her part came a further disenchantment, born of the inability of husband

---

[151]A brand of champagne.

and wife to find a common ground of interest. The habits and migrations of the sand grouse, the folklore and customs of Tartars and Turkomans, the points of a Cossack pony—these were matter which evoked only a bored indifference in Vanessa. On the other hand, Clyde was not thrilled on being informed that the Queen of Spain detested mauve, or that a certain Royal duchess, for whose tastes he was never likely to be called on to cater, nursed a violent but perfectly respectable passion for beef olives.

Vanessa began to arrive at the conclusion that a husband who added a roving disposition to a settled income was a mixed blessing. It was one thing to go to the end of the world; it was quite another thing to make oneself at home there. Even respectability seemed to lose some of its virtue when one practised it in a tent.

Bored and disillusioned with the drift of her new life, Vanessa was undisguisedly glad when distraction offered itself in the person of Mr. Dobrinton, a chance acquaintance whom they had first run against in the primitive hostelry of a benighted Caucasian town. Dobrinton was elaborately British, in deference perhaps to the memory of his mother, who was said to have derived part of her origin from an English governess who had come to Lemberg[152] a long way back in the last century. If you had called him Dobrinski when off his guard he would probably have responded readily enough; holding, no doubt, that the end crowns all, he had taken a slight liberty with the family patronymic. To look at, Mr. Dobrinton was not a very attractive specimen of masculine humanity, but in Vanessa's eyes he was a link with that civilisation which Clyde seemed so ready to ignore and forgo. He could sing "Yip-I-Addy"[153] and spoke of several duchesses as if he knew them—in his more inspired moments almost as if they knew

---

[152] Now called Lwiw, in the Ukraine, but at the time a city in the Austro-Hungarian Empire.

[153] Very popular song (full title "Yip-I-Addy-I-Ay") by Will D. Cobb (lyrics) and John H. Flynn (music), first performed in 1908 in the musical *The Merry Widow and the Devil*.

him. He even pointed out blemishes in the cuisine or cellar departments of some of the more august London restaurants, a species of Higher Criticism[154] which was listened to by Vanessa in awe-stricken admiration. And, above all, he sympathised, at first discreetly, afterwards with more latitude, with her fretful discontent at Clyde's nomadic instincts. Business connected with oil-wells had brought Dobrinton to the neighbourhood of Baku; the pleasure of appealing to an appreciative female audience induced him to deflect his return journey so as to coincide a good deal with his new aquaintances' line of march. And while Clyde trafficked with Persian horse-dealers or hunted the wild grey pigs in their lairs and added to his notes on Central Asian game-fowl, Dobrinton and the lady discussed the ethics of desert respectability from points of view that showed a daily tendency to converge. And one evening Clyde dined alone, reading between the courses a long letter from Vanessa, justifying her action in flitting to more civilised lands with a more congenial companion.

It was distinctly evil luck for Vanessa, who really was thoroughly respectable at heart, that she and her lover should run into the hands of Kurdish brigands on the first day of their flight. To be mewed up[155] in a squalid Kurdish village in close companionship with a man who was only your husband by adoption, and to have the attention of all Europe drawn to your plight, was about the least respectable thing that could happen. And there were international complications, which made things worse. "English lady and her husband, of foreign nationality, held by Kurdish brigands who demand ransom" had been the report of the nearest Consul. Although Dobrinton was British at heart, the other portions of him belonged to the Habsburgs,[156] and though the Habsburgs took no great

---

[154] "Higher Criticism" was the innovative and therefore controversial historical-critical method applied to Biblical studies by German scholars such as Friedrich Schleiermacher, David Friedrich Strauss, and Ludwig Feuerbach in the late eighteenth and early nineteenth centuries. It became known in England thanks to George Eliot's mid-century translations of Strauss and Feuerbach.

[155] Confined; the term is used of birds.

[156] i.e. he was a subject of the Austro-Hungarian Empire.

pride or pleasure in this particular unit of their wide and varied possessions, and would gladly have exchanged him for some interesting bird or mammal for the Schoenbrunn Park,[157] the code of international dignity demanded that they should display a decent solicitude for his restoration. And while the Foreign Offices of the two countries were taking the usual steps to secure the release of their respective subjects a further horrible complication ensued. Clyde, following on the track of the fugitives, not with any special desire to overtake them, but with a dim feeling that it was expected of him, fell into the hands of the same community of brigands. Diplomacy, while anxious to do its best for a lady in misfortune, showed signs of becoming restive at this expansion of its task; as a frivolous young gentleman in Downing Street remarked, "Any husband of Mrs. Dobrinton's we shall be glad to extricate, but let us know how many there are of them." For a woman who valued respectability Vanessa really had no luck.

Meanwhile the situation of the captives was not free from embarrassment. When Clyde explained to the Kurdish headmen the nature of his relationship with the runaway couple they were gravely sympathetic, but vetoed any idea of summary vengeance, since the Habsburgs would be sure to insist on the delivery of Dobrinton alive, and in a reasonably undamaged condition. They did not object to Clyde administering a beating to his rival for half an hour every Monday and Thursday, but Dobrinton turned such a sickly green when he heard of this arrangement that the chief was obliged to withdraw the concession.

And so, in the cramped quarters of a mountain hut, the ill-assorted trio watched the insufferable hours crawl slowly by. Dobrinton was too frightened to be conversational, Vanessa was too mortified to open her lips, and Clyde was moodily silent. The little Lemberg *négociant* plucked up heart once to give a quavering rendering of "Yip-I-Addy," but when he reached the

---

[157]Vienna's Schönbrunn Park, beside the imperial palace of the same name, included a zoo.

statement "home was never like this" Vanessa tearfully begged him to stop. And silence fastened itself with growing insistence on the three captives who were so tragically herded together; thrice a day they drew near to one another to swallow the meal that had been prepared for them, like desert beasts meeting in mute suspended hostility at the drinking pool, and then drew back to resume the vigil of waiting.

Clyde was less carefully watched than the others. "Jealousy will keep him to the woman's side," thought his Kurdish captors. They did not know that his wilder, truer love was calling to him with a hundred voices from beyond the village bounds. And one evening, finding that he was not getting the attention to which he was entitled, Clyde slipped away down the mountain side and resumed his study of Central Asian game-fowl. The remaining captives were guarded henceforth with greater rigour, but Dobrinton at any rate scarcely regretted Clyde's departure.

The long arm, or perhaps one might better say the long purse, of diplomacy at last effected the release of the prisoners, but the Habsburgs were never to enjoy the guerdon of their outlay. On the quay of the little Black Sea port, where the rescued pair came once more into contact with civilisation, Dobrinton was bitten by a dog which was assumed to be mad, though it may only have been indiscriminating. The victim did not wait for symptoms of rabies to declare themselves, but died forthwith of fright, and Vanessa made the homeward journey alone, conscious somehow of a sense of slightly restored respectability. Clyde, in the intervals of correcting the proofs of his book on the game-fowl of Central Asia, found time to press a divorce suit through the Courts, and as soon as possible hied him away to the congenial solitudes of the Gobi Desert to collect material for a work on the fauna of that region. Vanessa, by virtue perhaps of her earlier intimacy with the cooking rites of the whiting, obtained a place on the kitchen staff of a West End club. It was not brilliant, but at least it was within two minutes of the Park.

The Baker's Dozen

Characters:

MAJOR RICHARD DUMBARTON

MRS. CAREWE

MRS. PALY-PAGET

Scene—Deck of eastward-bound steamer. Major Dumbarton seated on deck-chair, another chair by his side, with the name "Mrs. Carewe" painted on it, a third near by.

(Enter R. Mrs. Carewe, seats herself leisurely in her deck-chair, the Major affecting to ignore her presence.)

Major (turning suddenly): Emily! After all these years! This is fate!

Em.: Fate! Nothing of the sort; it's only me. You men are always such fatalists. I deferred my departure three whole weeks, in order to come out in the same boat that I saw you were travelling by. I bribed the steward to put out chairs side by side in an unfrequented corner, and I took enormous pains to be looking particularly attractive this morning, and then you say "This is fate." I *am* looking particularly attractive, am I not?

Maj.: More than ever. Time has only added a ripeness to your charms.

Em.: I knew you'd put it exactly in those words. The phraseology of love-making is awfully limited, isn't it? After all, the chief charm is in the fact of being made love to. You *are* making love to me, aren't you?

Maj.: Emily dearest, I had already begun making advances, even before you sat down here. I also bribed the steward to put our seats together in a secluded corner. "You may consider it done, sir," was his reply. That was immediately after breakfast.

Em.: How like a man to have his breakfast first. I attended to the seat business as soon as I left my cabin.

Maj.: Don't be unreasonable. It was only at breakfast that I discovered your blessed presence on the boat. I paid violent and unusual attention to a flapper all through the meal in order to make you jealous. She's probably in her cabin writing reams about me to a fellow-flapper at this very moment.

Em.: You needn't have taken all that trouble to make me jealous, Dickie. You did that years ago, when you married another woman.

Maj.: Well, you had gone and married another man—a widower, too, at that.

Em.: Well, there's no particular harm in marrying a widower, I suppose. I'm ready to do it again, if I meet a really nice one.

Maj.: Look here, Emily, it's not fair to go at that rate. You're a lap ahead of me the whole time. It's my place to propose to you; all you've got to do is to say "Yes."

Em.: Well, I've practically said it already, so we needn't dawdle over that part.

Maj.: Oh, well—

(They look at each other, then suddenly embrace with considerable energy.)

Maj.: We dead-heated it that time. (Suddenly jumping to his feet) Oh, d— I'd forgotten!

Em.: Forgotten what?

Maj.: The children. I ought to have told you. Do you mind children?

Em.: Not in moderate quantities. How many have you got?

Maj. (counting hurriedly on his fingers): Five.

Em.: Five!

Maj. (anxiously): Is that too many?

Em.: It's rather a number. The worst of it is, I've some myself.

Maj.: Many?

Em.: Eight.

Maj.: Eight in six years! Oh, Emily!

Em.: Only four were my own. The other four were by my husband's first marriage. Still, that practically makes eight.

Maj.: And eight and five make thirteen. We can't start our married life with thirteen children; it would be most unlucky. (Walks up and down in agitation.) Some way must be found out of this. If we could only bring them down to twelve. Thirteen is so horribly unlucky.

Em.: Isn't there some way by which we could part with one or two? Don't the French want more children? I've often seen articles about it in the *Figaro*.

Maj.: I fancy they want French children. Mine don't even speak French.

Em.: There's always a chance that one of them might turn out depraved and vicious, and then you could disown him. I've heard of that being done.

Maj.: But, good gracious, you've got to educate him first. You can't expect a boy to be vicious till he's been to a good school.

Em.: Why couldn't he be naturally depraved? Lots of boys are.

Maj.: Only when they inherit it from depraved parents. You don't suppose there's any depravity in me, do you?

Em.: It sometimes skips a generation, you know. Weren't any of your family bad?

Maj.: There was an aunt who was never spoken of.

Em.: There you are!

Maj.: But one can't build too much on that. In mid-Victorian days they labelled all sorts of things as unspeakable that we should speak about quite tolerantly. I dare say this particular aunt had only married a Unitarian, or rode to hounds on both sides of her horse, or something of that sort. Anyhow, we can't wait indefinitely for one of the children to take after a doubtfully depraved great-aunt. Something else must be thought of.

Em.: Don't people ever adopt children from other families?

Maj.: I've heard of it being done by childless couples, and those sort of people—

Em.: Hush! Some one's coming. Who is it?

Maj.: Mrs. Paly-Paget.

Em.: The very person!

Maj.: What, to adopt a child? Hasn't she got any?

Em.: Only one miserable hen-baby.

Maj.: Let's sound her on the subject.

(Enter Mrs. Paly-Paget, R.)

Ah, good morning. Mrs. Paly-Paget. I was just wondering at breakfast where did we meet last?

Mrs. P.-P.: At the Criterion,[158] wasn't it?

(Drops into vacant chair.)

Maj.: At the Criterion, of course.

Mrs. P.-P.: I was dining with Lord and Lady Slugford. Charming people, but so mean. They took us afterwards to the Velodrome,[159] to see some dancer interpreting Mendelssohn's "songs without clothes."[160] We were all packed up in a little box near the roof, and you may imagine how hot it was. It was like a Turkish bath. And, of course, one couldn't see anything.

Maj.: Then it was not like a Turkish bath.

Mrs. P.-P.: Major!

Em.: We were just talking of you when you joined us.

Mrs. P.-P.: Really! Nothing very dreadful, I hope.

Em.: Oh dear, no! It's too early on the voyage for that sort of thing. We were feeling rather sorry for you.

Mrs. P.-P.: Sorry for me? Whatever for?

Maj.: Your childless hearth and all that, you know. No little pattering feet.

Mrs. P.-P.: Major! How dare you? I've got my little girl, I suppose you know. Her feet can patter as well as other children's.

Maj.: Only one pair of feet.

Mrs. P.-P.: Certainly. My child isn't a centipede. Considering the way they move us about in those horrid jungle stations, without a decent bungalow to set one's foot in, I consider I've got a heartless child, rather than a childless hearth. Thank you for your sympathy all the same. I dare say it was well meant. Impertinence often is.

---

[158] Luxury restaurant opposite Piccadilly Circus in London.

[159] Possibly the Alexandra Palace Velodrome in north London, built 1902. Intended as a place of popular recreation, it was never as successful as had been hoped.

[160] Punning on Felix Mendelssohn's series of piano works "Songs Without Words".

Em.: Dear Mrs. Paly-Paget, we were only feeling sorry for your sweet little girl when she grows older, you know. No little brothers and sisters to play with.

Mrs. P.-P.: Mrs. Carewe, this conversation strikes me as being indelicate, to say the least of it. I've only been married two and a half years, and my family is naturally a small one.

Maj.: Isn't it rather an exaggeration to talk of one little female child as a family? A family suggests numbers.

Mrs. P.-P.: Really, Major, you language is extraordinary. I dare say I've only got a little female child, as you call it, at present—

Maj.: Oh, it won't change into a boy later on, if that's what you're counting on. Take our word for it; we've had so much more experience in these affairs than you have. Once a female, always a female. Nature is not infallible, but she always abides by her mistakes.

Mrs. P.-P. (rising): Major Dumbarton, these boats are uncomfortably small, but I trust we shall find ample accommodation for avoiding each other's society during the rest of the voyage. The same wish applies to you, Mrs. Carewe.

(Exit Mrs. Paly-Paget, L.)

Maj.: What an unnatural mother! (Sinks into chair.)

Em.: I wouldn't trust a child with any one who had a temper like hers. Oh, Dickie, why did you go and have such a large family? You always said you wanted me to be the mother of your children.

Maj.: I wasn't going to wait while you were founding and fostering dynasties in other directions. Why you couldn't be content to have children of your own, without collecting them like batches of postage stamps I can't think. The idea of marrying a man with four children!

Em.: Well, you're asking me to marry one with five.

Maj.: Five! (Springing to his feet) Did I say five?

Em.: You certainly said five.

Maj.: Oh, Emily, supposing I've miscounted them! Listen now, keep count with me. Richard—that's after me, of course.

Em.: One.

Maj.: Albert-Victor—that must have been in Coronation year.
Em.: Two!
Maj.: Maud. She's called after—
Em.: Never mind who's she's called after. Three!
Maj.: And Gerald.
Em.: Four!
Maj.: That's the lot.
Em.: Are you sure?
Maj.: I swear that's the lot. I must have counted Albert-Victor as two.
Em.: Richard!
Maj.: Emily!
(They embrace.)

The Mouse

Theodoric Voler had been brought up, from infancy to the confines of middle age, by a fond mother whose chief solicitude had been to keep him screened from what she called the coarser realities of life. When she died she left Theodoric alone in a world that was as real as ever, and a good deal coarser than he considered it had any need to be. To a man of his temperament and upbringing even a simple railway journey was crammed with petty annoyances and minor discords, and as he settled himself down in a second-class compartment one September morning he was conscious of ruffled feelings and general mental discomposure. He had been staying at a country vicarage, the inmates of which had been certainly neither brutal nor bacchanalian, but their supervision of the domestic establishment had been of that lax order which invites disaster. The pony carriage that was to take him to the station had never been properly ordered, and when the moment for his departure drew near, the handyman who should have produced the required article was nowhere to be found. In this emergency Theodoric, to his mute but very intense disgust, found himself obliged to collaborate with the vicar's daughter in the task of harnessing the pony, which necessitated groping about in an ill-lighted outbuilding called a stable, and smelling very like one—except in patches where it smelled of mice. Without being actually afraid of mice, Theodoric classed them among the coarser incidents of life, and considered that Providence, with a little exercise of moral courage, might long ago have recognized that they were not indispensable, and have withdrawn them from circulation. As the train glided out of the station Theodoric's nervous imagination accused himself of exhaling a weak odor of stable yard, and possibly of displaying a moldy straw or two on his unusually well-brushed garments. Fortunately the only other occupation of the compartment, a lady of about the same age as himself, seemed inclined for slumber rather than scrutiny; the train was not due to stop till the terminus was reached, in about an hour's time, and the carriage was of the old-fashioned sort that held no communication with a corridor, therefore no further traveling companions were likely to intrude on Theodoric's semi-privacy. And yet the train had scarcely attained its normal speed before he became reluctantly but vividly aware that he was not alone with the slumbering lady; he was not even alone in his own clothes. A warm, creeping movement over his flesh betrayed the unwelcome and highly resented presence, unseen but poignant, of a strayed mouse, that had evidently dashed into its present retreat during the episode of the pony harnessing. Furtive stamps and shakes and wildly directed pinches failed to dislodge the intruder, whose motto, indeed, seemed to be Excelsior;[161] and the lawful occupant of the clothes lay back against the cushions and endeavoured rapidly to evolve some means for putting an end to the dual ownership. It was unthinkable that he should continue for the space of a whole hour in the horrible position of a Rowton House[162] for vagrant mice (already his imagination had at least doubled the numbers of the alien invasion). On the other hand, nothing less drastic than partial disrobing would

---

[161] (Latin) higher; upwards.

[162] A Rowton House was a hostel for working men (named after their originator, Victorian philanthropist Lord Rowton).

ease him of his tormentor, and to undress in the presence of a lady, even for so laudable a purpose, was an idea that made his ear tips tingle in a blush of abject shame. He had never been able to bring himself even to the mild exposure of open-work[163] socks in the presence of the fair sex. And yet—the lady in this case was to all appearances soundly and securely asleep; the mouse, on the other hand, seemed to be trying to crowd a Wanderjahr[164] into a few strenuous minutes. If there is any truth in the theory of transmigration, this particular mouse must certainly have been in a former state a member of the Alpine Club. Sometimes in its eagerness it lost its footing and slipped for half an inch or so; and then, in fright, or more probably temper, it bit. Theodoric was goaded into the most audacious undertaking of his life. Crimsoning to the hue of a beetroot and keeping an agonized watch on his slumbering fellow traveler, he swiftly and noiselessly secured the ends of his railway rug to the racks on either side of the carriage, so that a substantial curtain hung athwart the compartment. In the narrow dressing room that he had thus improvised he proceeded with violent haste to extricate himself partially and the mouse entirely from the surrounding casings of tweed and half-wool. As the unraveled mouse gave a wild leap to the floor, the rug, slipping its fastening at either end, also came down with a heart-curdling flop, and almost simultaneously the awakened sleeper opened her eyes. With a movement almost quicker than the mouse's, Theodoric pounced on the rug and hauled its ample folds chin-high over his dismantled person as he collapsed into the farther corner of the carriage. The blood raced and beat in the veins of his neck and forehead, while he waited dumbly for the communication cord to be pulled. The lady, however, contented herself with a silent stare at her strangely muffled companion. How much had she seen, Theodoric queried to himself; and in any case what on earth must she think of his present posture?

---

[163]With a regular pattern formed by holes.

[164](German) A year spent travelling abroad, especially before taking up a profession.

"I think I have caught a chill," he ventured desperately.

"Really, I'm sorry," she replied. "I was just going to ask you if you would open this window."

"I fancy it's malaria," he added, his teeth chattering slightly, as much from fright as from a desire to support his theory.

"I've got some brandy in my holdall, if you'll kindly reach it down for me," said his companion.

"Not for worlds—I mean, I never take anything for it," he assured her earnestly.

"I suppose you caught it in the tropics?"

Theodoric, whose acquaintance with the tropics was limited to an annual present of a chest of tea from an uncle in Ceylon, felt that even the malaria was slipping from him. Would it be possible, he wondered, to disclose the real state of affairs to her in small installments?

"Are you afraid of mice?" he ventured, growing, if possible, more scarlet in the face.

"Not unless they came in quantities. Why do you ask?"

"I had one crawling inside my clothes just now," said Theodoric in a voice that hardly seemed his own. "It was a most awkward situation."

"It must have been, if you wear your clothes at all tight," she observed. "But mice have strange ideas of comfort."

"I had to get rid of it while you were asleep," he continued. Then, with a gulp, he added, "It was getting rid of it that brought me to—to this."

"Surely leaving off one small mouse wouldn't bring on a chill," she exclaimed, with a levity that Theodoric accounted abominable.

Evidently she had detected something of his predicament, and was enjoying his confusion. All the blood in his body seemed to have mobilized in one concentrated blush, and an agony of abasement, worse than a myriad mice, crept up and down over his soul. And then, as reflection began to assert itself, sheer terror took the place of humiliation. With every minute that passed the train was rushing nearer to the crowded and bustling terminus, where dozens of prying eyes would be exchanged for the one paralyzing pair that watched him from the farther corner of the carriage. There was one slender, despairing chance, which the next few minutes must decide. His fellow traveler might relapse into a blessed slumber. But as the minutes throbbed by that chance ebbed away. The furtive glance which Theodoric stole at her from time to time disclosed only an unwinking wakefulness.

"I think we must be getting near now," she presently observed.

Theodoric had already noted with growing terror the recurring stacks of small, ugly dwellings that heralded the journey's end. The words acted as a signal. Like a hunted beast breaking cover and dashing madly toward some other haven of momentary safety he threw aside his rug, and struggled frantically into his disheveled garments. He was conscious of dull suburban stations racing past the window, of a choking, hammering sensation in his throat and heart, and of an icy silence in that corner toward which he dared not look. Then as he sank back in his seat, clothed and almost delirious, the train slowed down to a final crawl, and the woman spoke.

"Would you be so kind," she asked, "as to get me a porter to put me into a cab? It's a shame to trouble you when you're feeling unwell, but being blind makes one so helpless at a railway station."

FORTHCOMING

Saki:
The Complete Annotated Short Stories

The only full edition of the short stories, including the fifteen stories missing from other 'collected' editions, with an introduction and explanatory notes.